FOREVER FAITHFUL

DANIELLE KATHLEEN

❀ Created with Vellum

To my husband,
Who sat and watched many documentaries with me on this subject.
Your encouragement and enthusiasm is priceless, your support
means the world to me.
I love you.

HAPPY BIRTHDAY LIZ

A sudden dip of the airplane startled me and I clung to my armrest. I leaned my forehead against the window, watching the night sky glide past, like the tail of a shooting star. Somewhere below, the Seattle skyline appeared, and I pressed my nose up against the cool glass, my big eyes widening as I took in the beauty of the city. The Space Needle stood proud and tall, standing over the city like a glowing beacon of hope and aspiration, as if it were beckoning me to come closer.

I was giddy with excitement, my heart racing as the plane descended into Seattle. I ran my fingers through my SoCal bun in anticipation of exploring the city that once housed a musical revolution. Brant sat next to me, squinting out of our small window before giving up and turning back around. A smile spread across his face when he saw me looking at him, and he leaned forward to press his lips against mine.

"Thank you," I whispered between gentle kisses.

I nestled into his shoulder. This trip had been on my bucket list for years, but I never expected my husband to make it happen. Somehow, though, he had remembered every detail from the conversations we'd shared months ago about what I wanted for my birthday.

THE EDGEWATER HOTEL was a series of connected buildings built right over the water, so that we had to walk out the back door onto a pier before reaching the main building. Brant told me it was the only hotel in the world constructed like this. Two other hotels on the shore, both recreational resorts, but neither of them were built over the bay like the Edgewater. We'd reserved an expensive room with a king-size bed across a magnificent rock fireplace that ran up to the ceiling. I walked around the corner from the bathroom, admiring the view of Elliott Bay at night. The calm waters rippled and sparkled with the moonlight. I was living a reality I had seen on Discovery a dozen times, fantasizing staying in a place and affording a place like this.

Now it all made sense to me how we could afford this trip. Brant had been working tirelessly, spending long hours teaching online classes and tutoring students to make extra money. We had been saving every penny, putting it away for the future upgrades to our home or if I could persuade him, anything to help with the IVF treatment.

He brought up the trip a few days ago as a surprise, when he wanted me to open my birthday card early. I saw the printed emails of the plane tickets inside, the hotel and map of sites he knew I wanted to visit. That meant a substantial chunk of savings was gone. My mind immediately couldn't help itself. The IVF would have to wait.

I embraced him. Thanked him and realized quickly, he did this for me. I needed to be grateful. I was, but now worried about the extra expenses.

Brant already had us unpacked. It was the first thing he did when we traveled. He needed to feel settled and hated living out of a suitcase. He wandered over, towered over me and his arms wrapped around my waist and his lips planted soft kisses on the back of my neck.

"You know we can walk around naked? No interruptions," he whispered in my ear. As intrigued as I was, the first thing I thought about was our boys back home This was the first trip we were without them. A slight tinge of excitement and yet guilt pulled at my heart strings. All I could think about was how much they would enjoy the view and bug us to go swimming or fishing.

Brant picked me up in his strong arms and cradled me onto the white feathery comforter of the temper-pedic bed. His hands unbuttoned my pants hungrily. I peeled off his fitted t-shirt from his body. His excitement pressed against me as he pulled away from kissing me, whispering he wanted me to lay back and relax while his kisses travelled down my body.

LATER THAT NIGHT, up in the hotel, I knew the other hotel guests could hear Brant and me arguing. Our voices were projected and having alcohol in our system only escalated our emotions.

"Why do you have to bring this subject up?" Brant tossed his blazer on the cream upholstered bench at the end of the bed.

The four glasses of wine, lobster tail and fillet minion made me agitated and painfully full. We have been arguing from the steak house, the bar and now up to our room. When we got this way, we didn't care who heard us.

Holding the door slightly ajar, when I took a look into hallway. I saw a few guests pass by with concern, or whisper to one another.

My uneasy apologetic smile as the door closed was hopefully to give them the right signal of just two people having their regular marital argument.

"Brant, please! Keep your voice down!" I didn't think I did any favors for myself.

He paced the room with his hands on his hips. He was in the coach soccer mode as he kept his words inside, when usual he was arguing mentally on what to say. Our marriage therapist spelled that out for him in the last few sessions. Brant was afraid to share because he thought it would push me away and he and the boys will be alone.

With my hands on my hips, I stood at the door. Waiting for him to say something.

"I didn't mean to bring it up. I just saw the couple with their baby and I just…want something like that." My words jumbled.

The argument between us was a repetitive loophole because neither one of us would back down from the other's final decision. I wanted children, of my own. I loved the boys, but I was missing this internal motherly instinct of creating, carrying and delivering my own baby.

What I loved about Brant, he was a blunt son of a bitch. What made our marriage get to these points, he wasn't willing to compromise.

His hand jackknifing in the other to point out as he finally collected his thoughts.

"We have been over this, Liz. We can't afford the treatment."

No matter how many times he tried to be rational about our finances, knowing on two teacher's salaries we couldn't afford the invetro fertilization. It stung, every, damn, time.

"We were saving money and then you go and plan this trip, wiping us nearly out! You knew what I truly wanted to save for, but there are always excuses, isn't there!"

The vision of him blurred as the tears pooled in my eyes.

My body is shaking from the aggression I was holding back from the restaurant.

In our pasts arguments, the opportunist that I was. I wanted to take out loans and figure things out later, just as long as I could carry and have a child of my own.

As a reminder and a realist, Brant had to point out, he couldn't fathom financial hardship on a possibility I could miscarry.

When we first got together, I was honest and told him about my desire to have a child. I suffered from bicornuate uterus. As a teenager, it was a hard pill to swallow and understand my uterus was a heart shape, not pear. I could get pregnant, but I could never carry to full term.

Knowing I wanted a child, Brant shared he would consider the idea of IVF treatments when I had the surgery to correct my uterus. A year in a half later, I was moved in with a small gold band on my wedding finger and we were playing house.

At thirty years old tomorrow, I felt my clock was ticking. A woman's chances drop over thirty percent by the time they turn thirty. With my monthly friendly reminder of mother-nature, my yearly pap smear appointment is monitored, and my reproductive system was beginning to do the opposite, I wasn't producing as many eggs as I should.

So, I panicked. My own research on my uterus made me slip into a depression because now I was racing an internal clock. Private loans were out of the question because the interest rates were too high and we didn't have the forty-percent down payment.

All I thought about was how I wanted to be pregnant and have all the kids as close in age as I could. Then, last year Brant and I got pink-slipped from the school district. As teachers were constantly in jeopardy because of teacher strikes, union strikes, parent strikes. It was a never ending battle and our finances suffered.

"I just wish for once you saw this as a gift, not a burden!" I yelled at him as I struggled to take off my poor choice for high heels.

My feet swelled and standing near the fire place, holding the mantle for support. Brant came over to help me I snapped at him that I had it.

"Liz, we are just getting back to being comfortable again. Each year the popularity of this procedure increases by six percent. Can you believe it? We'll never be able to afford it."

With one heel off, I breathed a sigh of relief. "We could take a second out on the mortgage."

Deep down I knew it was a terrible idea, but I was desperate. Brant's mouth nearly dropped.

"Are you insane? I only have ten years left on my house. I'm not about to refinance and increase the rates. The interest rates are going up, that's dumb."

The next heel came off. I sighed as the pressure released and he thought I was at an understanding with him, not my heel. Both feet flat on the cold tile in front of the fire place, stung and throbbed. I know I expressed the pain on my face, because Brant's expression changed from looking at me like a crazy woman to a concerning husband.

"You told me that we could have a baby!" I snapped.

"We have two boys. That is plenty—"

I growled at him as I stomped over to the bed to undress. I was pissed when he brought up the boys. He knew I was forever grateful to be apart of their lives, but he refused to see it my way.

"I want to carry my own. I want to give birth to something beautiful that we created."

There was no reasoning with him. He continued to shake his head and be so damn stubborn about this.

"All you'll do is complain. You'll be uncomfortable, bloat, gain weight, and have weird cravings."

For some reason, he felt the need to point this out and as I call mansplain to me how I didn't think about the steps of being pregnant.

I struggled to tear off my black panty hose. I huffed and gritted my teeth, as I listened to Brant point out more reasons why I would feel uncomfortable being pregnant. I went to say something, but Brant raised his voice. Unlike him, I cared about our neighbors on either side of us.

He continued to point it out. "The mood swings and since we can't do this the less cost-effective way, you'll have to endure those shots, be monitored and the risk is too high for you to miscarry."

He followed me to the bed to point out in his usual manner on his fingers. My blood was boiling at this point and I couldn't even look at him as I struggled, yet again on the zipper of my dress.

"Liz, if we were financially stable—"

"You would still try to convince me otherwise, wouldn't you?"

When I spun around, I could see the regret on his face. We both hated to fight about this, but there was something he was holding back.

"You thought because you brought two boys to the table that I would change my mind? Didn't you?"

His gaze left mine down to the floor and back up to meet my teary eyes. "I thought at one point we were ready for this but—"

All I could hear was his excuses on how to dance around what he felt and not the truth. I stormed into the gorgeous all white marbled bathroom and slammed the door. Neither one of us wanted to say the inevitable, but Brant didn't want me to go through the procedure because he didn't want anymore children.

On the other side of the door I heard him slam some drawers and yell at me that he was going out. My birthday weekend was going to be a long one.

SPACE NEEDLE

I couldn't get the stupid dress to unzip. I cried on the bathroom floor for hours and at one point crawled out of the bathroom, made it to the feathery soft white linen bed and fell asleep. In the morning, I could feel Brant's long and heavy muscular arm wrap around my waist and scoot himself closer to me. We both lay in silence for what felt like hours as the dawn light just peeked into the room with the orange glow.

His warm breath comforted the back of my neck. He always made me feel safe and secure. I tightened my eyes, resisting the urge to cry. I hated how he could get over things so quickly.

In our therapy sessions, I was working on how to let go. Not hold in anger. In return my free arm smoothed over his and his grip on my waist tightened more. I could feel him needing what he felt he knew how to do best. Brant was a passionate and incredible lover. I know that's why I easily fell in love with him. My body was a temple and he knew how to make my toes curl just by his soft kisses. His lips knew how to caress my skin as he suckled and teased.

When we fought, he always needed time to cool off, take a walk for a few blocks then come back to me. He always figured the next best thing was make love to me.

Where I should have been strong and held my moral ground, I could never resist him. It was wrong for both of us to use our love making as a forgiving emotion, but I ached for his touch and how he looked at me when he made love, was like I was the only woman he ever needed.

"I'm sorry." I heard his morning husky voice whisper as his lips touched the back of my neck. "This is your birthday weekend. Can we just not bring it up and discuss it when we get home?" The tone was so damn sexy, I was already melting.

Instead of a response. I nodded, holding back the tears. My sniffles gave me away and he rolled me over and his muscular body cradled onto mine. He was being gentle and sweet with me with his tender touch. He didn't want me upset, and in between kisses he apologized for yelling. He asked for forgiveness as his lips kissed my ear, caressed down my neck, across my cheek and onto my lips. As his kiss deepened, he moaned, wanting me to feel his length between my thighs.

"I was a jerk. Let me make it up to you."

He continued to kiss down my neck and his fingers found a way up my dress and between my thighs. I gave into him willingly, because I needed his touch and tongue to make it all better. He did a few times over.

TODAY IS, my actual birthday. Last night was not a great start, but I wouldn't allow the argument ruin the rest of the weekend he planned. After our room service, he had an UBER driver take us to the Space Needle.

The view from the top of the Space Needle would have been breathtaking, but with the gloomy clouds, we couldn't see much of anything. I stared out from the three-hundred and sixty-five degree window panes into the dense and thick fog.

"Thank goodness they have a bar up here."

Brant came back with two glasses of mimosas in champagne flutes.

A part of me found this day comical because I knew how hard he planned, and seeing a few documentaries on Seattle, the views from the film makers were beautiful and spectacular, but we got nothing but gray, thick and ugly fog.

"The view from below our feet is scary."

Our eyes glanced down to the see-through floor beneath us. We were up about five-hundred and eighteen feet from the ground. As the thick clouds faded in and out below, We could see the people below wander around like lost ants. Some people avoided standing on the tempered glass as it slowly in the three hundred, sixty-five degree turn.

Brant and I drank our mimosas as we stared out and see as much as we could, which was dismal. The glass didn't lift from our lips until the last droplet landed onto my tongue.

"Time for the Chihuly Gardens?" He said.

The sarcasm in his tone made me playfully push him away. I set my glass on the bar counter as we walked toward the elevator to take us down to the gardens.

What I adored about my husband, he hated to be late for anything. My arms wrapped into his. We both were feeling the effects of taking the elevator down with the mimosas as my head was light as air and I couldn't stop laughing. By the time we were at the bottom floor, I was nearly stumbling as Brant was trying to hold me up and laughed with me.

"Now, this is going to be good."

Brant discovered that we were walking in the wrong direction as we were crossing the lawn and found himself an employee. He was worried we would miss the tour since we were having trouble locating the building. What didn't help our cause, we couldn't stop laughing and Brant fumbled a few words.

Cutting through the lawn, on her break or next shift, an elder woman favoring her right side as she walked holding a canteen was stopped when Brant asked her if she knew if we missed the last tour.

Bothered to answer us in our giddy, slightly intoxicated manner, she had as much personality as Grumpy Cat. "Wow, you almost missed the only tour we give once a year." Her steady, sarcastic tone displayed as she noisily chewed on a breath mint. "Go to your left and then a sharp right…"

We went to leave, but she wasn't finished. "You'll see your tour guide, the happy go lucky, Pat…He is tall…" She took a good look at my six-foot two husband. "Yep, I think taller than you. Any questions?"

Even if we had any, before we opened our mouth, she walked away from us carrying her canteen mumbling under her breath.

PAT, SEEMED just as eager to give the tour as the woman who helped us. She was correct on the fact he was taller than Brant. He was thin with big features to his face and matching lips, that I don't think he smiled too often as his bottom lip almost came out in a pout.

The famous Beatles style, mop-top black hair was the only thing Pat had going for him. Even the patches of facial hair he tried to grow, showed me he didn't try very hard. His white crinkle polo shirt with the Chihuly Garden's logo had some stains from his lunch, and his crinkled pants was clearly the best this kid could do for himself.

He spoke into a headset in a monotone voice and towered over everyone.

"Good afternoon ladies and gentlemen. I'm your tour guide, Pat. No, it's not short for Patrick. My parents were idiots...from the South...the Deep South. Yes, you can feel sorry for me, but only after I give you this tour."

Brant and I cracked a smile. We understood the kid's humor. Both of us knew a tour like this, as energetic as Pat was, this was going to be pure entertainment as sarcasm was our second language.

As we all followed, Pat did a head count and roll call. When he couldn't pronounce the first or last name, he made those people stay in the back and said to blame their parents for giving them lame names that no one could pronounce.

"Ah-Nah-Ees?" Pat said, looking up from his clipboard, irritated.

The roll of his eyes when the young girl too busy watching videos on her phone, but with enough sense to respond to her name made Pat mumble into his headset.

"Typical." Was a word I was able to understand coming from his mumbling.

When Pat called my name, I raised my hand as though I was in grade-school with the eagerness of knowing the answer to a difficult problem. Brant wanted to laugh but covered his mouth. My arm came down slowly as all eyes turned in my direction.

Pat's eyes narrowed over his clipboard and slid down his long nose. "You have a question, Liz?"

Embarrassed, I wish I could erase this moment. Even in school I had the problem of being a know-it-all. My hand always shot up, like there was an urgency. Growing older, adults didn't need to raise their hands like an eager child. Especially in a crowd like this.

What was more embarrassing, I rose it so quickly, I felt my body sway. I was still a bit tipsy from the alcohol and instead of laughing it off, I could feel the heat of my body rise, with my cheeks and ears turning red.

"No…" My voiced cracked.

"Then why did you raise your hand?" As the tour fell into silence, Pat speaking into the microphone intensified.

"How about we carry on." Brant spoke up to break the awkwardness.

"Don't tell me…" Pat looked at his clipboard. "Brant, I'm assuming."

The sarcastic tone was no longer friendly with my husband. He didn't know where Pat's angle was going. Brant stood up straight, easily sizing up Pat. His stern face focused in Pat's direction. He wasn't a man to be messed with, knowing in Brant's fraternity days of partying, wrestling, his way of having fun was fighting.

Pat saw the stare. He was no match for my husband and decided to continue on with the tour and mumble into his headset.

"Maybe your name is short for Brat…or something of that dumb hippy nature,"

What Pat was not aware of, with my husband's previous college days, his hearing was a bit impaired. Brant didn't exactly hear the mumble.

He leaned down to my ear as we followed people. "He say something?"

I shook my head. "I didn't hear anything."

Brant smiled and pulled me close to kiss the top of my head. "Liar. Punk is lucky."

"We're on vacation. Let's not end up in jail."

"Then why did we even come to this place? I planned on

complaining about it being over-priced, dirty food, foul language, being robbed and get some jail time."

The sarcasm in his tone made me smile. I saw the concern in fellow strangers, because a lot of people didn't understand Brant's humor, like I did.

TAKEN

I was in complete awe as the artwork of the ornate blown glass was staged in eight massive scenes. The black back drop that surrounded the sea life tower of swirling colors of blue, and greens. The yellow color represented the sea creatures of squid, starfish, shells and sea urchins.

Artwork like this in the glasshouse, I admired. Seeing art like this made me wish I had a sliver of this kind of vision and talent. I was by no means an art expert. Blown glass, paintings of landscapes, or portraits was my type of art, but this, was breathtakingly beautiful.

The forty foot tall glass and steel structure easily covered over four-thousand feet of light filled space. The one-hundred foot long sculpture of red, yellows, oranges and amber were different shades of a vision of a floral arrangement. When the sunlight could peak through the clouds, the illuminated colors mirrored an image on the floor.

The unique avant-garde gardens took patience and admiration, something Brant had trouble with. He was easily distracted but couldn't wait to walk into the next scene. I would rather take my time and stand and admire the many hundred of hours it took to imagine a scene like this.

Distracted from walking through the yellow and orange giant floral pieces hanging from the ceiling, I received a phone call from home. It was my mother, informing me that my youngest, Steven, is sick with a cold.

Being this far away from him, made me dread about being on vacation and not by his side.

"Hi honey...grandma tells me you are not feeling well?"

His small, eight-year-old voice spoke with a stuffy nose.

"I don't feel well. You coming home and bringing me soup?"

This pulled at my heart strings all the way from Southern California. My hand went over my heart at the sound of his voice, question, and he thought to talk to me first made the guilt in my heart ache. My little boy sounded even smaller like a four-year-old. I stepped away from the group to be able to hear him. A group of foreigners came toward us and spoke in what I assumed was German.

One German male approached me and asked for information in English, but his accent was thick. I didn't understand why he would ask and I'm sure the confusion on my face didn't make it easier. Another woman approached us and guided the German's and pointed in another direction.

"I'm sorry, they were confused because my uniform is the same color as your jacket."

She walked back over to her group.

Steven coughed into the phone a few times and I told him I would bring me a little gift from Seattle. He wanted something from the beach. He loved collecting seashells.

"Alright, any size?"

He lingered on the idea by thinking out loud as he hesitated. I felt I could visually see him think long and hard on this, because he knew it had to be the best one.

"Can it be the biggest one you can find?" The excitement in his tone screeched through the phone.

"Of course!" I promised him.

When my mother jumped back on the phone, we went over again the timing of our flight back home and how long she needed to stay at the house.

Brant glanced over at me because I was missing part of the tour. I held up my index finger to let him know to give me a minute. Pat continued on, seeing me on the phone and didn't seem to have a care in the world.

I loved the woman dearly, but she was someone who enjoyed their private time and space. She wasn't irritated, Brant told me last night how he had this trip planned six months in advance and every month had to remind her of taking care of the boys.

I was thankful because she truly did love them as though they were her own biological grandchildren. She was the one who told me to not be afraid of being a step-parent. I wasn't afraid, I just knew that with the boys' mother not in the picture, a lot of the burden was left on me.

"I love you." There was a strange tone to her voice.

"I love you too mom, call if you need anything."

Something felt different. It was in her tone with a longing that didn't seem right. Like, I was going to hear it for the last time as I hung up the phone.

The tour was wrapped up and I missed the ending. A crowd of people approached Pat for questions that he clearly was in no mood for still speaking into the microphone with yes and no answers.

In the distance, I saw the woman helping the Germans and I took notice we both wore black pants, white dress shirts and even though she had a blue blazer and me a blue petite coat, I understood the coincidence. She gave a quick smile and walked through the exit of the exhibit and into the gift shop area with the group, translating for them.

Brant waved me down already with toys in hands from the gift shop. I saw him stare at the translator and do a double take, when I approached he looked back at her and then me again.

"That was weird." He gave a questionable look.

"What?" I followed his eyes toward the translator.

"You two not only dressed a like, I think we found your doppelgänger. You didn't notice?"

I searched for the woman again to give a second look.

"No…Hold onto this incase Steven calls. He isn't feeling well and needs the biggest seashell from the beach for his collection. I need a restroom."

I handed Brant my phone as my eyes searched for public restroom sign. I felt the sudden urge, reminding myself I had been holding it for too long.

Pat was signing off. We were asked to not ask any more questions because he made it clear he had to take his regulated lunch break. As he was making his way through the crowd that no one bothered to ask him anything, he stopped in his tracks and his Adam's apple bobbed heavily when Brant stood in his way, immediately intimidated.

"But, if you have a question—" He spoke into his headset.

"My wife needs the restroom." Brant took a step closer to Pat.

Pat pointed in the direction behind him. "Around the right corner from the notebooks."

He and Brant made eye contact for a few more seconds. No one knew what was going to happen next. Brant stepped aside with a smirk on his face and allowed Pat to walk by.

"Bully." Pat said underneath his breath. Brant did not hear.

"I'll be back down in a few minutes."

I pulled Brant close and gave him a kiss on the lips. A few other people clapped and thanked him for putting Pat in his place.

When I rounded the corner, there was a line waiting outside the door at least thirty people deep. I got the attention of an employee about to walk by and asked if there was another bathroom nearby. He pointed to the outside doors and told me there was another set in the next building, but a large school field trip just broke out. Seeing the disappointment on my face, he leaned in to whisper about the other stalls across the field toward the gardens. It was a few yards away, but because of it being near the gardens, few people knew about it.

I RUSHED OVER AS quick as I could, through the path and over the small bridge and sure enough. A small cement building tucked near the caged fence I found to be sketchy but then relieved at the same time. My body took over to rush in and quickly undress. On my tip-toes bouncing from one foot to the other, I literally did the pee-pee dance on my way in.

The door handle to the woman's restroom was locked. I huffed in disappointment. *Of all the times!* My palm smacked the door. The men's restroom was right next door. *It's not against the law!* I was dancing around as my bladder was ready to burst. *Oh for goodness sake! They have the same toilets!* I argued with myself.

Then I went ahead and opened the men's restroom door with ease and stepped inside.

Pure joy and relief escaped my voice as I hovered the toilet. I held onto my yoga pants to steady my balance. Then I heard screeching tires off in the distance. *Am I near the parking lot?* I pulled up my pants, hesitating to leave the stall.

Living in Southern California can make one a bit on the uneasy side. Now being in Seattle, in unknown territory, I felt the goosebumps form on my body as I could have sworn the rumbling of a muffler was right outside this small concrete building.

This made my heart race in my chest. My stomach tightened, there was something about the sound that didn't feel right. I went to pull my cell phone from my purse, but forgot I gave it to Brant. Two car doors screeched open. I heard heavy footsteps from the back of the building.

The voices outside mumbled, were deep manly voices. My heart pounded in my chest. I breathed heavier and soon realized that I was being loud. I sucked up my air and closed my lips to breathe from my nostrils.

The finger-tips of my right hand rested on my stall door. *As if you are strong enough to hold the door back with one hand?* I gave myself attitude. *Now you are being silly! They could be waiting for someone, they could work here.*

I took a deep breath and let it out. I needed to get over this strange feeling and get back to Brant. He was probably worried about me. There was no way to get a hold of me and I didn't even bother to tell him where I went.

Shaking off the worry to get out of this small building, I marched quickly to the sink to wash my hands. When I went to dry them on the paper towel, I heard a voice shush the other and then there was silence. My anxiety wanted to get the best of me. I took my time and dried my hands on the paper towel. A knot formed in my throat. I couldn't shake off the bad feeling in the pit of my stomach.

My hands shook as I reached for the door handle. I recalled when I rushed in, I locked the door behind me. I suddenly became calm and felt like an idiot. My shoulders relaxed, and I thought about how silly I was.

I unlocked the door to step outside, I didn't want to make

eye contact. I pulled the strap of my purse on my shoulder and tried to B-Line to the path and back into the building.

"Rebecca?" A man's voice came from the back of the building.

Why I stopped myself and turned around, I did on instinct. It was the sound of his voice, like he commanded me. The knot seized in my throat. The fear spread down my body. Seeing the stature of this man dressed in all black. The size of him grew as he came around the van. His bushy black beard and light blue eyes seared into my mind for the few seconds. When he moved one hand from behind his back, something long and black like a baton.

Say something! "I'm sorry." I shook my head. "You have the wrong person." My voice trembled.

"Got her."

The husky voice behind me made my heart stop. Before another thought came into my mind to react, my head tried to spin around as quick as I could make it, but something dark went over my head and the beautiful scenery of the dark clouds, trees and gardens was gone. Within seconds, my arms went behind my back, my hands quickly secured listening to the zip-tie cut off my circulation to my hands.

"No!" I screamed, trying to pull away from the man behind me. His grip was too tight.

Oh God! Oh God! "Help me!" I pleaded.

The sudden rush of adrenaline, even having my face covered, I felt the the presence of the male figure rush toward me. A fist went right into my stomach knocking all of the wind out from my body.

I wondered many times in my life what it would feel like to be punched in the stomach with such force, air escaped as quickly as it halted to come back into my lungs. I dropped to my knees on instinct and wanted to curl up into a ball.

"Quick! We have forty seconds left!" One of them panicked to the other.

Four sets of hands picked up my body. Two at my feet and two at my shoulders. I gasped for breath. I could not get my mouth to register to my lungs that I needed air.

"Come on, man, that wasn't necessary," I heard one voice say near my head.

It didn't sound like the man who said the name. His voiced had a slightly higher pitch.

I gasped loud and my body finally felt the air suck back into my lungs and reacted with greatness as my heart raced the blood through my body. Finally my instincts kicked in and I thrashed my legs all around, slipping, falling, but I couldn't tell where.

"This one is strong," a deeper, harsher voice said.

One of them grabbed struggled with my legs as I kicked. I felt the grip of his hands try and grip to secure but how I thrashed around and kicked back, it made it difficult.

He cursed at me to stop. I kept kicking, but his firm grip on my ankles around my boots squeezed to the point I felt numbness begin to trickle in my calves at the loss of circulation.

The hands carrying me at my shoulders were losing their grip. Both of them were having a difficult time controlling me. My upper body twisted and my legs kicked to push off of him. I nailed one guy in the chest with both feet and my head struck the other guy in the chin.

As their grip released me, I didn't think about the aftermath. I landed on the concrete floor, my heading hitting hard.

Groggy, the right side of my body immediately numb and tingled on my hips, shoulder and head. A ringing in my ear traveled through my head, I caused more damage to myself and was pissed.

Was I breathing? I couldn't tell. I was in too much pain and the ringing in my ear wouldn't subside. I couldn't hear anything. My body lay limp on the cold concrete.

Their presence wasn't around me. I didn't feel anyone as I tried to roll over on my back.

Could they have given up? Someone catch them in the act? Could it have been Brant? Did he finally find me?

As my senses came to, they were there, just arguing. The sound of their feet shuffled around echoed in my head. The man at my feet laughed. The other man near my head kicked me in the stomach. I lost all strength. My stomach and lungs were out of sync. The pain was unbearable.

"Stupid bitch!" The shuffle of his feet indicated he wanted to kick me again, but he was stopped by the other man.

"Ease up man. She got one over on us, that's all. Remember, they aren't suppose to come in damaged." One of them said.

"You put her in the van then!" He spat.

A pair of hands scooped me up, the weight of me was limp. My head bobbed the few short paces, and then I was tossed and felt a padding of something soft like thick foam. The hands placed on my left side flipped me over to be deeper inside, then I heard one side of the doors shut.

"What about her belongings?" One of them said.

The other door shut and I didn't hear his response. As my head throbbed in pain, there was only silence left.

NOT ALONE

My legs were burning from having to control what balance I could in the back of the padded van. I wasn't easily thrown off from my previous gymnastics and snowboarding days. What made this a touch difficult was not being able to see anything and not knowing when the van would turn. The challenge was my hands were zip-tied behind my back. I solely relied on my legs for balance.

When there was a sharp turn, a few times my face smacked against another padded wall. I was trying to regain my composure. From floor to ceiling this van was padded with something very thick. The rumbling of the muffler was like a kitten purring. It was faint, but still something.

The van came to a slow stop, I sat on my knees and shook the bag off my head. Fresh air compared to the CO2 I was inhaling was refreshing. My lungs reacted as I took in longer breaths. I was in pure darkness. No windows, not even a small crack of light. Then, a sudden turn nearly knocked me on my side, but I regained and my body moved with the van.

Having lost a sense of time fueled my anxiety. Each

passing second made my mind race with fear of what they planned on doing with me. My mind fought at the terrible thoughts of what they wanted from me. How could I handle being possibly beaten, raped and kept captive?

My breathing grew heavier at the thought of my outcome. I was a big fan of crime shows. My reality, the scenario of me living through something like this, wasn't good. Taken in daylight, in a public place, these guys didn't stumble, didn't show eagerness. They were mad I nearly got the better of them, but they were calculated.

I felt my abduction could have been planned. But, why me? This is not how I wanted to spend my thirtieth birthday.

I sank to my butt and held myself as close to the wall as I could. My bottom lip quivered as the images and ideas these sick men would want with me. I struggled with the idea of the many women I saw on the crime shows end up in fields after being tortured or raped and how I would hate Brant to see me like that.

How my family would have to live with the fact that something happened to me in such a violent manner. My head pressed into the padding as hard as I could, because I needed to feel pain and concentrate on that, over the hundreds of thoughts of what could happen to me.

More than anything, I wanted this to be a sick joke. A stupid and poor attempt to scare me straight. At what? I couldn't fathom a reason why, which made my reality creep in with the bad images again.

This can't be how I spend my birthday!

My body felt the change in the transition. The ride was now smooth and steady. *We must be on a freeway.* Before they could have been doing donuts in a parking lot for all I knew to throw me off. Little did they know, just being in Seattle, I was a foreigner. I already had trouble with a sense of direction. I wish I knew how I was in this horrible mess in the first place.

Brant told me in his fraternity days, they would do this for initiation for new comers. On a small level, I wanted this to be the answers to my prayer. *Please let this be a sick joke!* As if my head wasn't in enough pain, I lost my emotions and started to sob. *Of course he would never do this to you!* My heart ached for my husband. I couldn't imagine what he must be going through.

Why couldn't you have waited in that line? I was so angry with myself and my dumb decision. *Why didn't you tell him which bathroom you were going to? Why didn't you take him with you?* My nose was running, The tears rolled down my quivering cheeks like tiny rivers.

My breathing shallowed as I felt the vehicle slow down. The vibration was merely invisible. I sat up on my knees ready for my fate, whatever it may be. The vibration was still now. The van stopped.

My sore knees maneuvered over to the back doors. I stood up hunched over and off to one side. The right side of my head was in too much pain to lean against the padding. On my left I tried to hear anything of where I could be, or if something was wrong.

They have to open the back at some point. When they do, I needed to be ready. Staying at this end meant when the doors open, I could surprise them and kick them open, knocking them to the ground. Like an action hero would as I saw in movies.

Faint muffled sounds were outside the doors. I tried and strained to hear anything, but nothing came out clear.

Suddenly, I nearly lost my balance as something bumped into the van. I staggered, caught myself and went back into position. Adrenaline coursed through my veins like a sleeping giant had awaken inside of me. I geared myself up for something to happen, give myself a chance. My legs in a strong stance, my chest breathing heavy, waiting for my opportunity.

I heard the click of the handle and the grinding metal turn.

"Help me!" I shouted.

The fear shook from my body as my voice projected suddenly, it was a strange feeling as if I wasn't in control. I didn't know if anyone could hear me, but it was worth a shot.

The back doors to the van opened wide with force. Both men stood firm at the edge of the van, held angry faces with hard glares at me. The taller of the two appeared out of breath and suffered from a bloody nose, and his left eye was swelling. He spit blood on the ground.

I hated that I stiffened, no sound came out when I saw their faces and I froze with fear. Before I uttered a noise, the smaller man reached for my left foot and swept me off my feet. I fell on my left side and he put his tobacco smelling palm over my mouth.

"I'll slit your throat if you say another word," he barked at me.

I swallowed hard at the thought. I didn't know what these men were capable of. Both of them lifted a third male with a bag over his head off the ground. *Another victim?*

"Get in the back!" The smaller of the two men yelled at me.

Carefully, I rolled over to the other side. There was a large landscape of dirt and construction equipment stationed for the night. The moon was high in the clear night sky. There was no other sign of life beyond the dirt field. If I thought about running, they could easily snatch me back in the van. There was no where to run to. They both grunted as they shoved a man in the back.

I saw my moment to try and sneak out if I thought I could

be quick enough. The door to my side was slowly closing, if I waited another second and kicked it open, I could nail one of them and hopefully knock them both down.

The bigger of the two closed one side of the doors. He paused when we both made eye contact. It was how he stared at me, my skin easily tightened and wanted to shrivel. I could see the struggle in his light blue eyes. He wanted to do something to me. The wheels in his head spun with ideas as he gripped the side door, as his breathing grew heavier. If he was given the chance, within seconds he would pounce on me. My stomach tightened as the bile in my throat wanted to rise.

MY COMPANION

The smaller of the two kidnappers pulled a syringe out of his pocket, removed the cap with his teeth and injected the man with the bag over his head in the neck.

"You didn't get his hands?" The smaller man pissed at his partner.

This made the taller of the two snap out of his fixed trance on me, reach in his pocket to zip tie the man they tossed in the back of the van.

"That'll keep em' down for the count," the smaller man said as he spit the cap from his lips.

"She should be wearing the bag over her head." The bigger man said as he slowly turned in my direction.

"Who cares." The smaller man said with a chuckle.

He snatched my left ankle and pulled me closer to both of them. He laughed, seeing and feeling my fear.

"Look at this one."

He tugged harder and my right foot made contact with his chest. It made him loose his grip and threw him off balance, to land on his butt.

"Screw you both!" I yelled.

The bigger man laughed at his partner. Then, he rested both palms on the pad.

"You're not there yet. We could have some fun." His deep rough voice with ill intentions.

The smaller man pulled at his partner, dusting himself off in the same moment.

"What do you want?" I snapped.

Both of them looked on the sides of the van. I went to scream and the small of the two put his index finger to his lips. Neither one of them showed the slightest hint there might be a problem.

"You scream and Ozzy will have no problem having a go at you while me and this douchebag watch." His thumb pointed to indicate the taller man with the beard was Ozzy.

Ozzy grabbed himself to display his junk for me, incase I wasn't clear on what his intentions would entail.

"How about we settle the score now. I have to explain why I have a busted face. He grabbed the side door to jump in.

I scooted back with my feet and closed my mouth and thinned my lips. My eyes blurred instantly with tears.

"Please…" My dry lips quivered with a crack to my voice. "I have a family. Please let me go and I won't say anything."

Both men snapped their necks to look at one another wide eyed. In this few seconds of silence, if I could get them to change their mind, I could have a chance of survival.

"If this is about money, I don't want to disappoint, but I have none." I stammered. "Well, that's not true. I have a 401K, but I'll give you whatever is in it. You have my purse and I'll give you my pin to my ATM card, whatever you need but there isn't much."

Ozzy's eyes were big, he stood with his hands clenched at his sides. He stepped back to pace.

"Shit! Shit!"

Ozzy's chest was puffing out, like he needed to destroy something.

The smaller man of the two met Ozzy's small back and forth pace. He remained calm with Ozzy, trying to get him to cool down.

"It's alright! They won't know."

"He was very specific, we have been tracking her for weeks!" Ozzy snapped.

When Ozzy saw me again, he gritted his teeth. He grunted in frustration, stomped over and slammed the back doors in my face.

My heart weighed heavy in my chest. The tip of my nose tingled as I tried not to cry. I nearly forgot how to breathe in. Something was wrong with my kidnappers. I probably sealed my fate worse off than what I had been in.

The groan from the man near me had his face buried deep in the pad. With my knees, I helped adjust him as best as I could. When I heard a heavy sigh and then a snore, I knew he was going to be ok.

The back doors swung wide open again, which startled me, made my heart thump against my ribs. Ozzy stared at me with the bright full moon behind him. I couldn't explain why the beautiful clear night sky and moon illuminated my attention. My brain forced me to take a mental note.

This could be my last night alive.

Ozzy ruined my image, his face wasn't the last thing I wanted to remember. Whatever plan they had, I was clearly not supposed to be a part of it. He shushed the other man as he mumbled and looked back at me.

"You have children?"

I nodded.

"A husband?"

I nodded again. He scratched his head. He cursed under his breath.

"Sorry...Looks like we don't have a choice."

He slammed the doors.

"No!" I cried out. "Help me! Someone help me!"

My screams didn't do anything, except startle the man in the back of the van. He must have been so groggy from what they injected him with, he couldn't fully wake up and react, only mumbled in reaction.

I COULDN'T SLEEP like my companion. When the van drove off, I prayed that he wasn't hit hard enough with whatever they injected him with that he could have respiratory problems, and die in the back of this damn van.

The motherly instinct in me wanted to help. I leaned down from time to time to listen to him breathe. When I came to the conclusion he was alright, I would sit back on the other side.

My butt was going numb from sitting on it with my legs in an Indian style. I got up to only hunch and stretch out my legs.

Hours passed, which during the time I switched places, stood and leaned on the wall to try and stretch my back. Listening to my companion snore annoyed me to jealousy.

The van was a smooth ride and had been for hours. There were no more sharp turns, just straight motion with a soft and faint purr.

When my eyelids were heavy, I found myself nodding and bouncing back up to keep myself awake. I heard a deep moan from my companion. My body perked up listening as his breathing became harder and raspier. My eyes already adjusted to the darkness, I could see his faint shadow rise up on his knees and shake the bag from his head. He sat back on the other side of the van and breathed heavily.

"Shit."

He smacked the back of his head on the pad out of frustration.

Now I allowed too much time to pass between us. My mouth moved to say hello, but no sound came out. My mind was racing on what to say or do, to the point where a full minute went by. My body jolted when his feet banged against the floor.

"That's useless," I managed to stupidly say.

"Holy shit!" The startle from his voice was apparent. "I'm not alone?"

I felt bad I didn't say anything beforehand. "It's just the two of us."

There was a brief silence in air. His voice cleared. "Do you know the two guys who did this to us?"

I shook my head and then answered him realizing he couldn't see me.

"No. I was taken from the Space Needle area. You?"

"I was outside my new apartment. I just moved today. They parked in front of my moving van."

My heart leapt at the thought there could have been a witness.

"Was anyone helping you move?"

"No. I promised my girl I would move in the last bit of our stuff today."

For some reason, listening to his voice was a bit of comfort. It could have been because I was not alone. My head rested on the padded wall. I could only see my companion as a dark shadow. Fear crept in again on what was now, *Our* situation.

When I couldn't take the silence any longer, next best thing was introductions. "I'm Liz."

"Zak." He responded calmly. "They mention what they wanted?"

"Nothing. I mentioned my husband and kids. They didn't seem happy about that."

NOT A STRANGER ANYMORE

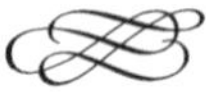

I couldn't help myself and every few hours, my emotions would burst and I would sob for about ten minutes and try and calm down. Zak sat in silence and didn't utter a word. He could be crying for all I knew, there was no way to tell. With the darkness surrounding us, I only heard my sniffles.

I was tormented on what Brant would be going through. My imagination conditioned me to visualize him running around, shouting my name, panicked he couldn't find my face. He would run up to someone in security, the police would be involved, and then he would be in the surveillance room. They could watch from where I left him.

I didn't even say I love you. Which caused me to tear up.

The surveillance crew would watch, trace my steps and I hoped there was a camera nearby.

What could be devastating was to watch my kidnapping. Brant would see how I fought hard as the bag was thrown over my head, he would see I tried. Then being kicked, picked up and tossed in the back of this van, would have him in a rage of emotions.

"The van has got to stop at some point." Zak spoke up. "They'll run out of gas soon enough."

I uttered a last sniffle. He was right to think like that.

"What are we going to do?" Hoping there was more to his words.

"I remembered a video I saw about getting out of zip-ties…We should see about getting these zip-ties off and give ourselves a fighting chance."

The eager in his voice gave me hope we could do something together and give ourselves a possibility at surviving. Both of us met in the middle of the van on our knees. I could feel his body tower over mine as his voice was above my head.

His instructions were calm and clear. On our backs, we slide our zip tied arms under our butts. I breathed in deeply not being the most flexible human. I struggled and managed to get from under my butt and relieved when step one was accomplished. Next step, wriggle my hands from out of the bottom of my feet.

"Do you need help?"

Zak was kind enough to help as he pressed my knees closer to my chest and encouraged me to keep going, breathe slowly.

"You always watch videos to get out zip-ties?"

I had hoped he would understand my sense of humor. When I heard him snicker, it made me feel slightly relieved.

"My girl learned self defense and made me watch all these videos and had me practice on her." He said.

Smart.

As I grunted my way through this. Zak's shadow appeared to move effortlessly.

The sad part was feeling the sweat from my forehead roll down my sides and toward my ears.

"Ok, when we escape, I promise to hit the gym."

I managed to squeeze my feet under my zip tied wrists that were cutting off my circulation. I sighed when I broke free and the immediate tingle from my hands as they rested on my stomach.

The van came to an abrupt stop. I felt Zak's body fall onto me, our face inches from smacking into each other. He apologized and quickly recovered to rise on his knees.

"Hold on." Zak whispered.

I strained my ears again trying to hear what was going on outside the van.

When nothing seemed to happen, Zak wanted us to continue.

"Now, with your teeth." He whispered, "I need you to move the zip tie where the point of the knot is in the middle of your hands."

My teeth gripped on the knot and maneuvered it over in the center between my thumbs.

"Got it!"

"That's great!" Pleased at my quickness. "Now I want you to feel your hip bones with each elbow."

I did as he instructed and told him I did.

"Now, as hard as you can," he scooted closer to me. "You're going to ball up each hand into a fist, bring your arms up and jerk them back toward your chest as fast as you can, do you understand?"

"Yes." I did what he said, but nothing.

I heard him suck up his deep breath and the rush of his movement and a small snap.

"You're turn," he said.

I tried again and grunted. I did it again and wanted to grunt out of frustration. My wrists ached and my balled fists were loosing their strength.

Zak scooted toward me and clasped my hands in his.

"I know you have it in you. Take a deep breath and with all the strength you have, give it everything."

I sucked up a deep breath. I found the strength. Thinking about being in Brant's arms again, tuck my kids in their beds and hold them. I took a deep breath, raised my hands as tight as I could, I balled up each fist.

When my arms came swinging down, every ounce of strength left my body. The full force of my swing came back down hitting myself in the stomach, and I heard the snap of the band with the immediate freedom of my wrists.

"Good, Liz…that's good."

He gave me the fatherly pat on the back, which I needed. He moved to his palms on the padded walls of the van, glide over, hoping to finding a seam or camera. He complimented the craftsmanship and how hard it was to find anything.

Naturally my thumb and middle finger went to my ring finger to feel and twirl around my one carat gold ring and band. The blood was rushing back into my hands and my fingers were swelled from before. I was thankful to touch my ring that was precious and dear to me.

My stomach rumbled and gurgled. Not knowing how much longer we had, the last thing I ate was a blueberry muffin at the Space Needle before going up the elevator. My mouth salivated, dreaming of the warm muffin in my hands, picking the muffin top first and taking a bite of the buttery treat. My stomach growl harder.

"Here."

Zak reached across and touched my palm. I felt a small wrapped item in my hand.

"They only took my wallet, but left everything else in my pocket."

It was some sort of nutrition bar. I could feel the softness wrapped in the plastic wrapper.

"How did you know?"

"I could hear your stomach from the back of the van." He joked. "I have another."

My eager fingers tore open one corner and nibbled a few bites to satisfy the emptiness in my stomach. My throat was dry because the nutrition bar tasted like a dry oatmeal with a chocolate chunk and dirt. I didn't care, it was the best thing in my hand.

"I normally don't eat these." The last bit of the food particles slid down my throat. "I'm cherishing every bite."

I heard Zak snicker from the other side of the van.

"I'm glad to hear it. Why don't you normally eat meal replacement bars?"

"I prefer the real food." I said, without a second thought. "Not saying this isn't real food, clearly it is. I just prefer to have a meal."

I wanted to take another bite, but I wrapped up the rest of the bar to savor for later.

"I'm not judging. I've been conditioned to like those now for the last few years. I hated them at first. With discipline and a good routine, I've been able to get used to them."

I heard the monotone in his voice, he still must be trying to convince himself.

"Thank you for sharing. You didn't have to."

I rested my arms on my knees with my back against the padded wall. My muscles were tensing up from the long drive, the anxiety of my fate, and the sleep deprivation wasn't doing my body or mind kindness.

"We're in this together. Plus, we need to keep up our strength." He said.

He tore his wrapper and eagerly took a bite from his bar. He softly chewed and gulped it down.

There was a brief moment of silence between us. It was hard for me to not saying anything. I heard him pound a fist against the padding behind him and on the floor. My other senses heightened, my ears perked up and I reacted by a jolt of shock.

I gasped naturally and hated how it came out. He should be able to react however he wanted.

"Sorry." Zak's voice was somber.

"No, don't be. It's dark in this box. We can't hear anything." I pounded my fist on the floor.

"When they put me in the back of the van, they didn't say anything?" He asked.

"If I scream, Ozzy will have a go at me while you and his partner watch."

Remembering the blue eyes from Ozzy's stare, my skin ran cold. Zak shuffled close to me.

"Listen, whatever comes our way, when I tell you to run, run."

I was surprised at his heroism, and wish I could basque in the adrenaline inside of him.

"Say it with me." He asked.

Before my lips parted, the back doors swung open. Our hands immediately held up as we were blinded by a bright white light.

NEW SITUATION

My eyes were burning from the bright light shining directly in the van. Something electric turned on and my first thought was a taser gun.

"Both of you on your stomachs and heads down!" Ozzy shouted.

I kept my eyes closed, they were not ready to adjust to the brightness. I did as I was told and sensed Zak did the same as his shoulders rubbed next to mine. There was a strong amount of heat radiating from the light. My eyes watered, the top of my head was slowly absorbing the heat.

"Stay down!"

Ozzy reached in, snapped up the bags that went over our heads and tossed it back down before he exited. The immediate relief from the heat was a blessing.

"Put the bags over your heads."

My hands shook violently to put the bag around my head. I was so terrified I wanted to throw up.

"No," Zak said.

Before the bag fully went over my face, I saw a large black

boot blocking my vision. I felt Zak rise up quickly to grapple and take the man down.

"Run, Liz!"

Quickly, my body sprang up, ready to dart and run. But Ozzy was quicker. I could barely see anything. A dark shadow rushed toward me. I felt the brunt force of a metal object strike my jaw. The strong sound of electricity. Zak cried out, and next thing I knew, it was pitch black.

THE PULSING in my ears woke me. The movement was rough and louder than before. There were metal sounds, a rolling of something I couldn't figure out. I wasn't ready to wake up, because I still wanted to go back to my dream.

I wanted to wake up in my hotel room, roll over in the king feather bed as the sheets engulfed my body, and see Brant standing near the bed with a room service cart filled with food, sweet treats and that desirous look he gave me.

As the sounds in my current state of being grew louder, my vision of my sweet husband and warm hotel room slowly faded. My eyes flickered open to my same current state of darkness.

On my back, I could somehow feel the space was bigger than the van, as the oxygen was cooler but not as quiet. I felt the padding beneath me, it was colder than before. I pushed myself up. A shift beneath my feet was rougher than before, like rolling on metals balls beneath me. I could feel the slight rocking back and forth with faint momentum.

My eyes fully adjusted, there wasn't as much darkness. It could be because the space felt bigger with my senses, but there was something about the space I couldn't make sense out of.

"Zak!" My hoarse, scratchy voice called out.

There was no reply. Gaining my balance on my tired and

weak legs, I slowly stood up. My arms reached up as far as I could stretch myself and I didn't feel a roof. I didn't have to hunch.

"Zak!"

I coughed and cleared my throat. The air was crisp, not stuffy from before as we were inhaling two people's CO2. My nostrils took in a deep breath. My hands carefully reached out in front of me with small, baby steps to feel my way around.

My mind getting a better sense of my surroundings, my ears perked. I recognized the metal on metal rolling sound.

You're on a train!

The padding was everywhere, but wasn't as thick. Cold iron bars stopped me in my tracks and I jerked my hands back. Reaching out again, my hands gripped the cold metal and slowly stretched out beyond to see if anyone was there or get a feel for something. Big solid wooden boxes smacked my knuckles and bent my hands in.

The thought of me being alone made my heart race and built anxiety in my chest. I panicked, hoping to hear my companions voice.

"Zak!...Zak!"

The last thing I could remember was getting struck by the end of something like metal. My mind raced how I got myself in this mess, how he might have been killed because he wanted us to have a fighting chance. I dwelled how I failed him.

I was no good to myself mourning the loss of someone I didn't really know. I had to pull myself together and figure this place out.

My older sister was always the brave one. I was careful and calculated all my life. She was adventurous and a thrill seeker. She always wanted me to step up and do something big for myself. The only time I did was when I wanted a baby for myself. Then I married a man who was just as careful and calculating, but with finances.

If she was here with me in this moment, she would want me to know how big this place was. She would try and climb the bars if she had to. She would find objects to stack onto. That was where I needed to pull my strength and think, what would Shannon do?

My hands followed along the iron bars and then hit a corner with padding. I was ready to start again and in my head I began counting how many steps it took to reach each corner.

Seven, eight, nine and ten!

My hands bumped into a corner. My right foot stepped on something soft that sunk into the padding. I heard a moan, I froze in place, and fell to my knees with excitement.

"Zak!"

My hands followed on the ground to reach his body. My fingers glided to touch a foot and then an ankle.

"Are you alright?" Hearing the sound of his groans was a relief.

"Liz?…" His faint voice fluttered out. "Liz?"

My tense shoulders dropped, a smile stretched across my face. It was Zak's voice, and I had never been so happy to hear a stranger say my name.

"Zak. Are you alright?"

Beneath us, a heavy jolt shifted roughly and I toppled onto my left side and felt the soft crunch of plastic bottles.

"What is that?" Zak was just as familiar with the sound. "Water?"

I gripped both bottles from under my ribs and handed him one. My fingers twisted the plastic top off, I carefully brought it up to my nose to sniff. There was no scent. My dry and cracked lips eagerly wanted to taste the liquid, but I refrained from gulping it down.

"No smell." My bottom lip touched the rim of the bottle. "Let me go first."

"No!" Zak insisted. I heard a swing and gulp. He moaned with pleasure so much so that it made me blush.

"You're safe, it's water."

I heard the water guzzle down his throat.

I drank slowly to savor as much as I could. I didn't know when we would get another bottle. My stomach growled as the water made its way into my stomach and yearned for something else, something to slowly digest. My hands patted down my pockets to feel for what was left of the nutrition bar.

"Shit!"

If I would have known they would take it from me, I should have ate the whole damn thing.

"Did they take the food out of your pockets?"

Next to me, I felt Zak's movements as he searched in his pockets. He sighed.

"Yep."

The heat from his body shifted as my left arm felt the cold draft, listening to him stand on his feet. The water bottle crunched in his hands and toss it off to the side. I heard the metal "ting" as the bottle top struck the bars in our new living arrangement.

My hands cupped my ears when I heard him scream out the word, DAMMIT! He paced around the room. His hands banged on the bars out of frustration.

"WHAT DO YOU WANT!" He yelled.

PRECIOUS CARGO

Being forced to live in darkness, the rest of my senses heightened. It was true, Zak's anxiety levels could be felt across the room. I slowly made my way to my feet. The mother in me wanted to let him know we were going to be ok, but I wasn't certain myself. His pacing and heavy breathing and him pounding on the bars made me clench my teeth.

A part of me wanted to comfort him, get him to talk to me. Somehow, that always felt like a betrayal to my husband. My eyes closed, trying to ignore and stay patient.

It was hard listening to his footsteps on the padded ground. On the walls, the musical sound his fingers made when he grazed the bars. His breathing grew heavier, when I listened to his exertion jumping up and down, trying to get a feel of how far up the ceiling was, he couldn't reach.

"Zak!" I snapped.

My hands held my head. I was feeling mad at this point as all the sounds of the rolling, the breathing, the tinging of the metal, I was about to snap. At this point, I would prefer the silence.

He said nothing, he stopped and he sat near me as he slumped down.

Then guilt crept into my mind how I snapped at him. I shouldn't have. Both of us were literally in the dark and were complete strangers.

"I'm sorry."

He took a deep inhale through his nostrils and let it escape his lips before he answered.

"Don't be. You helped snap me back into reality. I would have snapped at you long ago. You have a lot of patience."

My lips stretched upward. "A mother of two boys and I'm a school teacher. Patience is the number one requirement before credentials."

The comment made Zak laugh. "Very true."

Carefully listening to our surroundings, the sound of steel and metal squeaking, creaking, rolling wheels through slight vibration as our new living arrangement shifted and rustled.

"Where the heck is this train going?" I asked.

Nothing I had watched or had known made sense to me. I knew I was no one of importance and certainly didn't know this man. No one I knew was in Seattle. Which made me think back to when Ozzy realized I wasn't the person he should have taken.

"Your thoughts to our predicament?" Zak said.

I imagined he used air quotes, as he slowed his tone with the last word. I would have done the same.

"As far as I am aware. We have no connections. I have no money, there has been no ransom or demand. I'm not famous, I don't come from wealth."

"Same." He said.

"I'm not a political figure."

"Your husband in construction?"

"No. Both of us are teachers."

"Well, that rules out jealous husband." He moves to stand on his feet. "You two live in Seattle?"

"Los Angeles."

"Never been."

"It's crowded, dirty, don't believe the hype."

I heard the small laugh coming from Zak's chest. It was nice to make some light of our situation.

Zak seethed through his teeth and pounded on the walls.

"WHY?" He shouted out into the universe. "I don't understand, what is this all for?"

"Why are you screaming?" The headache that had been building in the back of my skull was beginning to make its round toward the front.

"I bet you there is a listening device or a camera in here."

"Zak...please." I begged. "I understand but..." My chest clenched tight as my voice shook.

Zak was right at my side, he felt around for my water bottle, opened it for me and wanted me to drink.

After a few sips. I hated feeling, my situation, everything about this damn place!

There was no right answer. Being kept literally in the dark was going to make us mad. The headache was not going to subside and I knew I needed sleep.

"I'm sorry, I'm just pissed." Zak seethed.

Knowing everything about our situation was a guessing game. The fear was no longer harboring in my chest. Now, I was angry because there were no answers.

MY HEART WANTED to leap out of my chest as my body jolted to the sound of Zak banging on the bars. He grunted and seethed through his teeth. The shadow of him appeared he was trying to pull at the bars. After his last grunt, he stomped over and sat on the other side of the wall, near me.

When his butt landed on the floor, a loud crunch from the crushed-up water bottle he tossed earlier was the only sound between us.

I pressed my lips together, I couldn't control the laughter inside my chest, I cupped my mouth.

"I'm sorry." I fought holding in my giggle as I bit my bottom lip.

Zak snorted on the other side. A few seconds later, both of us couldn't hold it in and burst into a heavy laughter.

"No. I deserved that."

After a good solid minute of laughing, he sighed. "If you haven't heard. I have no clue how to get out of here. This space is tightly secured and no doors or windows. I'll try climbing the bars again."

Standing up to stretch my legs, I realized my headache went away. I was relived because the sudden rush of having one like that hit me was nearly unbearable.

Then the only idea that struck me to help pass the time was try and get to know my companion. I thought about an easy approach as I leaned against one wall.

"You mentioned earlier you were moving today in your new place. Where did they grab you?"

"They snuck up on me. Grabbed me from behind. It was dark in my new place, I was just about to plug in some lamps when they approached."

Disappointed, I remembered he was knocked out and then injected with something that made him sleep. I was the only one who saw them.

Then his place being dark didn't make sense to me.

"Your place didn't come with lights?"

"No. It was a new build. I was going to install them."

"By choice?"

My comment made him snicker.

"Me, no. My girl didn't like any of the designs. She

annoyed them to the point they did what they could to pass inspection and left."

I pressed my lips together as my eyebrows raised in question. Again, I was thankful he couldn't see my facial expressions. So far, his girl sounded like a lot to handle.

"A woman like that knows what she wants."

I had to control my tone to sound somewhat sincere. I needed to come across like I understood a women like her. Not that I had anything to prove, but Zak was still a stranger and I needed him as a friend.

"That's one way of putting it."

Thankful once again, Zak couldn't see me bite my bottom lip as I held in the giggle from my chest. I coughed to throw myself off.

"How long have you two been together?"

"About six years," he said.

"Wow!" I sounded too entrained and shocked at that comment. "Good for you two."

"You and your husband?"

"Four years."

This made me reach for my band and ring, feel it on my ring finger. The touch of the single stone helped keep me calm.

"Total or you've been married for four years?" He asked.

"Total. He proposed a year into our relationship and six months later, I was his wife."

There was a brief moment of silence between us and I thought to jump in and ask something before he could.

"Six years is a long time. No wedding bells for you two?"

His tongue smacked against his teeth as he breathed in.

"That's a good question. I wanted to at first, but her dreams were always bigger and she wanted financial security and to be wealthy, so we could afford the perfect wedding."

I remained silent. I felt it best not to comment against

her. Already, she wasn't sounding like someone I would socialize with.

"She has expectations. Hard deadlines, but she keeps me on track." He tried to solidify.

Zak sounded like a broken record. I've seen this many times with parents over their kids I taught. A strong working woman was great to have, it shows balance and how women could achieve just as much as men.

The ugly side to a workaholic was a good portion of their time was missing out on what was important in their kids life, because it was about chasing the next million dollar dream.

"What does, Zak do?" I asked.

"Went to college for a business major. I now manage and flip houses as my girl thinks that's faster money. We have a small business we've been building up."

Again, I almost felt the need to ask him who he was trying to convince with his monotone answer. I thought I could take that information and put it in a place to ask later.

I took a sip of my water. "Any kids?"

"No. We've talked about it though."

I was jealous they could even talk about it.

"Don't wait. There will never be a right time."

"I can agree since you are speaking from experience."

My mouth opened to reveal more, but emotionally I wasn't sure if opening up how I already felt less of a woman was healthy at this stage in our dilemma.

"Liz, you ok?" He said with concern.

"They are my stepsons. I can't have children."

The brief silence between us made me wanted to crawl into a ball and take it back. I must have made it awkward, because what should he do with that information?

"I'm sorry." He said.

. . .

THE TIME WAS PASSING BY SMOOTHLY as Zak and I shared information and were open about our lives. Since we were strangers, there was no emotions attached, it was nice to be open and honest without feeling judgment. In fact, talking in the dark and not being able to see the expressions I felt was a new type of therapy, but I'll hold onto that million dollar idea for when we get out of this place.

The padded walls and floor on the train kept us in a fatigued state as the heat secured itself in our box. I was comfortable, but Zak mentioned how this place made him sweat.

Zak belonged to a family from construction. He was the only one who went to college to make it in business. He came from a long line of loggers, builders, electricians and welders. He didn't mind getting his hands dirty, but preferred to be behind a desk and use his brain. When he shared the family business, he spoke highly of each member and each one of them had a unique story.

It reminded me of my father's side of the family from Scotland. They are natural born story tellers and everyone involved had a unique gift or talent. There was pride in his stories and I was intrigued by each of them.

I couldn't help, but my mind wandered to Brant being in Seattle at the Police station answering questions, going crazy and having to make the phone calls to my family and repeat the story over and over on what happened. The thought tore at my heart and I gripped at my chest when my heart thumped harder and the knot in my throat formed.

How will he tell the boys? How will the boys take it? They already lost their biological mother, now me? My heart ached, tears slid down my cheek.

"You alright?" I heard Zak's soft faint voice across from mine.

After maneuvering my wedding ring and band around

my finger for comfort. I wiped my tears from my face. Pulling myself together as I straightened up.

"I'm sorry. I was listening but—"

"It's okay to think of your family too." He finished.

"Last night…or…I should say the last night I was with Brant, we argued…a lot…" I took a deep breath. "I would have to go through a corrective procedure and also IVF, but it's not always guaranteed. We don't have the money and Brant…logically won't take a loan or a second on the house."

Zak was quiet for a few more seconds before he said, he was sorry.

"Do you think he will think you left him on purpose?"

The thought tore at me as a knife to the gut. I didn't even think of that! Now Brant might have thought I might have wanted to run away from our problems. No! I couldn't go there.

BRANT

Brant's thumb and middle finger couldn't help but touch and rotate his wedding band. This strange reaction made him feel closer to Liz, like he could still feel her when he touched the band. He was wearing down as the days past and now his body molded itself to the chair.

It had been a few hours in the police station at Detective Blake Knight's desk, waiting for her to the eighth cup of coffee. *Or was it my ninth?* He lost count, disillusioned as the second day passed by as he sat day after day waiting for anything new. He wasn't sleeping, he couldn't. Being alone, in a hotel with Liz's clothes, bathroom items and smelling her when he walked in made his heart ache all over again. His knees were sore from falling onto them when he entered that hotel room.

Detective Blake Knight walked back to her desk from the break room with a cup of coffee in one hand and Liz's file under her arm. She walked with confidence, wore the resting-bitch-face attitude with her pulled back blonde hair.

She handed Brant the coffee and sat on the other side of

her desk. He could never tell what type of news she was about to share, but there looked to be something behind her hazel eyes.

Leaning back in her chair, her fingers intertwined and rested on her stomach. She eyes Brant and he constantly felt judged. He did everything she asked of him and had nothing to hide. Liz had watched enough crime shows to understand he would be suspect number one. He didn't want a lawyer, because he wanted the Seattle Police on his side.

She took in a deep breath, then leaned forward to rest her elbows on the desk.

"We are still waiting on the footage from the gardens."

If he could, Brant wanted to squeeze the cup in his grasp, but then deal with hot coffee. He held in his temper and didn't understand what was taking so long.

"Another excuse. Is this normal detective?"

This made her sit back, and observe his behavior. Her eyes drifted down to the coffee cup, hearing the squeeze of the styrofoam in his grasp. He released when he followed her eyes.

"I've worked other cases where the footage didn't take this long. We have asked they bring us as much about the day as they could."

"My wife doesn't have that time!"

Brant set the cup on her desk. He wanted to pick up her desk and flip it, but he knew it wouldn't help his situation. No one was moving fast enough for him, like they didn't care. On his feet he needed fresh air, listening to the phones ring off the hook, other officers dealing with other family's, Brant couldn't think straight.

"Mr. Thomas," Detective Knight stood on her feet, she suggested with her hand he stay calm. "I know how hard this is on you."

A few other officers took notice at Brant's posture. They

observed him cautiously, their hands at their hips and ready to remove their .9mm Glocks if necessary.

"Am I free to go?" He had enough.

With her open palm, Detective Knight suggested he could leave.

"If I hear anything, you'll be the first phone call."

Brant nodded and thanked her as he walked out of the station more pissed off than when he came in. They were supposed to have the footage to go over. *Why was there a delay!*

On the street he walked over to his rental car he needed to extend for another week. Two other officers having a casual conversation caught Brant's attention when he heard about the missing wife from the Chihuly Gardens. He stood near the passenger door with the key fob in hand, not wanting to walk out of ear shot.

"Knight thinks the husband got rid of wife number two."

"No way! He was married before?"

"Wife number one died in a car accident while pregnant. Basically, chose to save the baby over her own life. A year in a half later, he marries this woman and he admitted to arguing a lot, but they deeply loved each other."

Before the officers went into the station, one of them stopped the other.

"Oh, did you hear about that crazy conspiracy on social media about people gone missing?"

"Oh geez. I told you not to listen to that crap."

"No, seriously. Within the last year, more people have been reported missing in their mid-twenties."

"It's got to be that sex-traffic operation."

"Men and women in their mid-twenties? Come on. We know they are considered too old."

One officer opened up the door and they both entered continuing their conversation.

Brant would need to remember to look into that when he got back to the hotel. He clicked on the remote and the car beeped at him to signal it was unlocked. He went to step off the curb, but a hand on his shoulder suggested he turn around.

Detective Knight stood with one hand on her hip. As the wind drifted by, a few hairs got loose and out of place. Her fingers immediately corrected and tucked behind one ear.

"The footage dropped in my email box a few seconds after you left."

The red rim around Brant's eyes lit up. *They found Liz!* Then, by her hesitation, he braced himself for the news. "Detective, please…" His raspy voice broke. His tired, blood shot eyes pleaded.

Her hazel eyes dropped to the ground, she sucked up a breath. Her jaw clenched, she was agitated.

"You stated that you and Liz separated at one point because she needed to use the restroom, correct?"

He nodded, she continued.

"When Liz walks out of the building, there is no more recorded footage. The outside cameras to that side of the building were scheduled for maintenance."

Detective Knight bit her bottom lip. This information is detrimental to their case, and now they have to go back to look over the employees working that day.

It was the painful, washed over dread as his face lost all its color. His body slumped back and leaned on his rental car. It was her job to keep him hopeful, yet at this point both of them were losing valuable time.

"It's almost been forty-eight hours. A very slim chance she is alive at this point. I know you mentioned you had a happy—"

"Have." Brant interrupted with irritation. This wasn't the first time she was about to suggest Liz was already dead, or worse she stated when they first met if Liz might have ran off. "If you are going to suggest that Liz left me willingly…" He paused, nauseated at the thought. "What's next?"

"Detective?"

Brant spun around hearing a familiar voice. Thankful to see his brother-in-law, Julian rush out of a cab to catch their attention.

It had been a long forty-eight hours without him. He knew strings will be pulled as Julian is in the FBI.

Slapping Brant on the back for comfort, Julian removed a business card and immediately handing it over to Detective Knight while showing his FBI badge in the same process.

"It's alright, we'll find her."

"You must be FBI Agent, Dermer?" Detective Knight put her hand out for a shake. Julian shook her hand back and wanted to be up to speed what was going on.

"I was just about to show Brant the surveillance footage. Sadly, it's not much." Detective Knight wore her annoyance.

"If it's not too much trouble, I'd like to see how I could help with this case." Julian said.

Without a second thought, Detective Knight walked over to the front doors of her station.

"Follow me."

SHARING

My lips were drying, every second I didn't take a sip of water. My tongue searched for moisture to lick my lips, but I was so dehydrated, there was nothing to share. I was hard to try and stay asleep as the rocking and jumbled moments of the train track made me bounce and I woke up.

In one corner of our space, there was a bucket with what felt like a toilet lid. There wasn't enough supplements in my body to urinate or do anything else. The stress of the whole ordeal made my body want to keep everything it could.

The dry heat in the box was not doing us any favors. My petticoat jacket was now my pillow. It was getting hot where my stretch pants and long sleeve shirt didn't breathe enough to keep me cool. It kept in the heat.

I needed exercise of some sort and thought it better to decided to wander around. I heard Zak on the floor, trying to sleep and his stomach growled. This made me think of food and drinks and then my stomach would share the same sentiment.

My eyes adjusted to my surroundings, I saw Zak was a dark shadow, an outlining of his physique. He appeared to be in shape, tall and broad shoulders. At times in the shadows, I couldn't tell how long his hair was, but I imagined it short with a style in gel on top.

"Liz?" He called out to me.

"Am I doing it again?"

"mmm, hmm."

"Sorry."

Earlier he pointed when it got quiet, I tend to walk around and my feet drag and shuffle on the ground. We agreed to try and not annoy the other and when it came to a point, it was ok to say something.

I leaned against the bars. The cold of whatever metal they were made out of felt better than the foam below that kept in our body heat.

"Liz?"

"Ya."

I saw Zak roll to one side and prop his head up with his arm.

"What happened to Brant's first wife?"

I was thankful and knew what he was doing. We leaned on one another for distraction. We needed the memories of our lives outside the walls to give us the strength of hope.

"She was in a car accident on the 405 freeway. It was a five-car pile-up because a truck driver fell asleep at the wheel."

"Jesus."

Sharing this was beginning to feel a bit therapeutic somehow. As though, I could tell a version of what I knew and because Brant wasn't around or that I was shy to give my input, no one would judge me.

"At the hospital, the doctors couldn't stop the bleeding.

The baby's heart rate was dropping. Steven wasn't ready to be born, and would be a premature at only twenty-eight weeks. Before Brant could arrive, the doctors gave her a choice. She chose Steven."

"Dang." Zak's voice deepened at the thought.

"Brant showed up at the hospital, and found out he had a newborn son and lost his wife in the same evening."

I recalled being at the school and finding out Brant's wife was killed. I hadn't known him very well then, but the decision did take many of us by surprise.

"Was he ever mad at her, because he wasn't given a choice? Because he would have chosen her." Zak's tone was sympathetic. "I would have done the same."

"I came into the picture about a year later when he and I were set up on blind dates and later found out that we weren't the couple that was supposed to meet."

The memory warmed my heart and made my lips turn upward. Becoming an instant step-mother had its ups and downs. Brant always supported my decisions and I did the same for him.

"The boys are so young and impressionable, they need a mother in their life and I was there with open arms."

"Sounds blissful." Zak said. I could sense the smile on his face. "Did Brant know of your condition?"

"Brant was aware when we first dated that I could conceive, but my uterus is in a heart shape, which means I could not carry to full term, constantly having miscarriages."

I crossed my arms over my chest to conceal my discomfort at the on-going problem that was within me.

I could never shake this feeling that my body wouldn't allow me to have children. I decided to keep talking before Zak could ask another question.

"As a teenager, I had a soccer accident and was kicked in

the stomach. The intense amount of pressure had me crawling off the field. My parents rushed me to the hospital. They asked me to try and urinate and I felt like it was peeing acid. A few quarter sized cists ruptured on my ovaries. Once the MRI and ultrasound were done, I was told of my rare bicornuate uterus condition."

"Wow! What a way to find out." Zak said.

"Since seventeen, I've carried this heavy burden. One point I thought it as a blessing because I wasn't sure if I wanted to have children. College was fun and easy and before Brant, there were a few I dated and tried to overcome the odds."

"You tried to get pregnant?"

"I was pregnant a few times. It was the overwhelming feeling of how my body could create such a small miracle that I could call my own."

The palms of my hands lay on my stomach. Reliving the memory and the feeling of change in such a beautiful way.

"I miscarried both times. Both of them men wanted a woman who could bare them a child, not someone damaged like me."

"Hey..." Zak scooted closer. He put his hand on my shoe. "Don't go there. They were the problem, not you."

I trailed off, thinking of my boyfriend history and how each time they were disappointed and that look in their eyes of all the hope deflating.

"Brant was different because he already had kids," Zak said.

"Exactly. Brant came into my life and didn't want any more children, I thought I finally found the right man for me. A year later after dating, we married and were blissfully happy with the it being the four of us. Then, a few years ago, I learned about a procedure correcting bicornuate uterus and the successful stories when I attended a baby shower. For me it went from a 1.5% to a 75% chance once my consultation was completed. Opening my options for the possibility of having a child, excited me."

"As it would for any woman."

Zak was a good listener. I had never vomited my life like this to anyone. I truly believed sharing feelings without seeing expressions was an amazing therapeutic breakthrough for someone like me. Brant would never sit and listen to any story this long. Though, Brant would have tried to tear the place apart. He didn't do well in confined spaces or in the dark.

His heavy hand tapped my foot for support. When he lifted it off, I felt the heat leave my foot.

"So, Brant didn't like the cost." Zak help continue my story.

"The possibility, and emotional journey I tucked away, now burst open."

Remembering the last night I was with Brant, the yelling of our voices inside my head. I called him out on his bluff about not thinking about the possibility of me having our baby. Truly, there was no intention. He felt his boys were enough.

"The cost of the procedure wasn't covered by our insurance." I swallowed. "The IVF treatments and medications after the procedure wasn't covered. Everything would be out of pocket."

"Or do you think because of how he lost his first wife and risking your life, he was making the decision with you that he couldn't with his first wife?"

WOW! I thought.

"That is incredibly intuitive. I never thought of it like that before."

I felt foolish because Brant was sensitive about his ex-wife. If he mentioned her, I could take it one or two ways. I could brush it off and act like that would never happen, or be upset because he was comparing our situations and decisions.

"No one has put it to me like that."

MY HEAD RESTED on my jacket. On my right side, my eyes were day dreaming about being in Brant's arms on the park bench, watching the boys play in the playground. Listening to their laughter was pure joy from their hearts and it made me smile. The clear baby-blue sky and hot Southern California sun was picturesque. The soft green grass was just cool enough to walk on to avoid from over heating.

My wonderful moment slipped from my thoughts as a loud emergency alarm sounded. I sat up to cover my ears.

Zak scooted over to me, his hand on my shoulder.

"Liz! You alright?"

The sound was intensely loud, I could barely hear him next to me.

"I'm alright!" My voice croaked.

The noise was beginning to subside. The vibration of the cargo was starting to slow down. The sound was bearable and I uncovered my ears. Once the motion seemed to have come to a stop, we both stood up carefully.

We stood as close as we could with our arms touching. Prepared to have something happened as the silence was deafening on our space. The goosebumps formed on my body, as though I felt something was about to happen, but didn't know what it was.

A large 'Boom!' and both Zak and I were knocked off our feet and I landed on my back and he on top of me.

I could feel his breath on my neck and my body stiffened. Surprising he didn't have body odor. There was a sweat and musk scent to him. He told me he was sorry and jumped up to his feet as quickly as he could. He helped me to my feet, needing us to be prepared, but the waiting game was giving me anxiety in my chest and tightening with every second passing by.

BREAKING POINT

"What the hell is going on?" Zak pounded on the wall. "Hey! Let us out! Someone help us!"

I did the same and screamed as much as I could.

"Let us out!"

Nothing. After a few more minutes, our dry and cracked throats coughed and couldn't get loud or scream anything.

I heard his feet land on the padding, then a grunt from him and the bars rattled.

"What are you doing?"

"Finding a way out." Zak got a hold of the bars and grunted as he climbed. "If we climb up these bars, we are bound to find something."

The hope and enthusiasm was replaced from his fatigued state of mind. I didn't want to burst his optimism, but reality struck me hard.

My hand reached out to touch the bars and see what I could do. They were colder than usual and it was hard to grip on. Like they were turning into freezing pipes. I yanked my hand back in reaction and rubbed my hand on my pants to warm up my palm.

The cold didn't seem to bother Zak, he didn't mention anything.

"I'm nowhere near Ninja Warrior status. I would hate for you to have all this faith in me and I can't even do a pull up."

Hoping he understand my light comedy at a dark moment like this. It was inappropriate, but at this point I knew I was near the delusional mental capability of what we were in for.

The grunt from his voice as he climbed higher, then the slip and his curse as he slid down and fell right on his back near me.

Zak smacked the padding and cursed again.

"The bars above are greased with something."

He jumped up and smacked the bars with his hands. Both hands gripped and he shook them with fierce strength.

I stepped back, listening to this made me scared, it was loud. I covered my ears and sat on my knees.

"What is this for!" Zak yelled to the ceiling.

The settling of the bars being rattled. Zak gave up and stopped harassing them. Nothing but silence between the two of us and there was still no movement from the train.

We were starved, sleep deprived, fatigued and growing weaker. Since we have been sitting wherever we are, I felt a cold creep in slowly and it made me shiver. I wanted a blanket to cover me, but all I had was the padding that locked in one side of my body heat.

"Zak. Do you think we were brought out here to die?"

I fought my fatigue to try and stay awake. I wasn't making sense and too tired to correct myself. We avoided the topic of death. Deep down a fear would set in both of our minds, paranoia would make us mad. I had to know and needed him talking to keep me awake.

I pulled my legs closer to my body to feel heat. The shivers in my body made my teeth chatter. I tightened my lips so Zak wouldn't hear. Not that I didn't mind his company, I just didn't want him to think he had to take care of me.

Without thinking, I shivered and exhaled. My voice shook and the cold seemed to seep into my flesh and move in toward my bones.

"Liz?" Zak sounded concerned. "What's wrong?"

He scooted over and the back of his hand rested on my cheek. He sharply pulled back.

"Liz! You're freezing!"

He sat right next to me and wrapped one arm around my shoulders and rubbed my right arm to cause friction and heat my skin. He pulled my jacket and wrapped it over me.

The movement felt nice and I felt the skin on my arm begin to defrost. I was too weak to comment how nice he was, or that what he was doing was helping. I leaned my head on his shoulder and the comfort of his warmth made my eyelids heavy.

I heard him whisper to me we were in this together and he promised he would find a way out so I can go back to my husband and boys.

"I can't have you get sick on me."

I thought I heard Brant's voice. My lips turned upward at the thought of my family. Knowing Brant was next to me, keeping me warm sent me on a soothing dream and I was able to relax.

WHEN I FALL into a deep sleep, I do one or two things. I'm either a part of the journey and it feels real, or I am in darkness and remember nothing.

I thought I found myself in Brant's arms. He was standing

behind me with his arms wrapped around me. I could feel his strength, the rise and fall of his chest as he breathed into the back of my neck. My cheeks flushed as his lips drew down to kiss one of my favorite spots. My eyelids fluttered as my body pressed back into him, wanting him to hold me tighter.

Being in his arms always made me feel safe. It has taken me years to get over my trust issues and allow someone inside my head. He was the first man who loved me for all my flaws and didn't judge me. We're we perfect, no. We argued, a lot, but in the end he knew how to talk to me, share with me and it was how he held me tight. I could trust him.

The other men in my life saw me as the type of woman you could bring home to your mother. I was sweet, kind and very naive. I chose the wrong men over and over and thought if I played the good girl routine, it would always work in my favor.

Instead, I got good-looking guys that liked me at home, while they partied and slept around with women who had more of a wild side. Again, I am careful and calculating. I have wanted to be a wild child, but I thought about the danger around me. Growing up in a big city, you always had to have your guard up.

As I fell into a deeper sleep, I felt Brant and I were someplace warm. I felt the sun on my face but I kept my eyes closed. The ocean breeze was light as it drifted by us. My lungs inhaled a deep breath and when it escaped, I felt at peace.

The sound of a woman's voice in the faint distance screaming disturbed our peace. I wanted to open my eyes and react, but for some reason, I couldn't. Brant's arms gripped tighter around me, I was uncomfortable and struggled to get away, but I couldn't.

The woman's scream came closer and louder with my struggle. I didn't understand why Brant was this abrasive with me. Panic ran through my body, I couldn't get out of his grip of what was happening to me.

I awoke in a panic, rolled over to sit upright. I was in the darkness again and I could smell my familiar surroundings of the padded floor, that almost reminded me of a new car smell. Mix that in with the sharp sour of the steel bars and the sweet musk of Zak.

I breathed heavily as my heart pounded in my chest. Saliva rushed to my mouth as my stomach turned. On all fours, I crawled over to the corner with the bucket to throw up in as best as I could. My stomach and body lurched as I coughed. I had nothing to throw up, but my body felt like I had to get something out.

The headache danced on each side of my temples and behind my eyes. My fists pounded on the padded floor. I didn't want to cry, I was tired and frustrated of always crying. I spit out the last of my vomit.

"Liz, you alright?"

Zak's voice was close by, but he was kind enough to give me space.

Tears rolled down my cheeks at the sound of his voice and I was thankful not to be in this alone.

"No." I sobbed. "I'm tired and I want to go home!" I screamed. "I'm tired of not knowing!"

I allowed too much bottled emotions stay inside. Because of my optimism it took me so long to digest situations. I naturally blocked out negative to always try and remain positive. This was a major weakness I carried and it was hard for me to break from.

I should have cried this out, yelled, screamed, but what did I do? I waited for an answer, or a sign. I was failing myself, my husband, and family.

The scuffle of Zak's knees rushed toward me. He kneeled and rubbed my back. He said nothing and allowed me to cry it out, again. We were both exhausted and I felt there was no end in sight for us. I needed comfort and security and without my husband I was breaking. My body shook as the fear crept in. Zak held me tight and his strength was comforting, but it was not Brant's. The darkness was wearing on me.

I wanted to kick and scream and to be let out of this box. Zak gripped my shoulders and even though we were facing one another, I could only see his outline. His strong hands rested on my shoulders in a tight squeeze ready to shake me and snap back into reality.

"I need you, Liz," A firm jolt from him made me sucked up my tears. "It's you and me now. We have to count on each other."

"I can't." My cracked lips sore from talking with the salt of my tears.

"Where is that calm school teacher? I need her."

Seeing his outline, his broad shoulders had the definition of someone who worked out. His head did have short hair and his hair was a bit messy. I saw the edges of his square jawline. I wanted to reach out and touch his face, but snapped out of my delusion.

"I don't want to be your friend! I want my husband!"

I didn't want Zak to console me. I wanted Brant to be here with me and comfort me. Zak agreed, but told me that we were all that we had and we needed to stay strong.

My body weak from the lack of nourishments, and the agony of our situation was compiling one right after the other. I breathed heavy and didn't realize I was dead weight on Zak when he sat down with me and had me lean into him for support.

"Breathe with me, Liz," he instructed.

What else was there to do. He held tight and when I could

gather myself, together we inhaled through our noses and I exhaled through my shaky lips.

"We'll get through this, together," his husky voice said. "We will find a way back to your boys."

The loud sound and burst of air escaping the side cargo door was like a truck setting their air breaks. The metal sound of the doors unlocking and the grind of the metal moving as the large side doors moved from the center and outward.

Zak and I scurried to our feet. He stood in front of me like a protective shield, keeping me from harms way.

My eyes couldn't help but notice the pitch black sky with the beautiful stars scattering the sky. I had not seen so many stars in my whole life. You would never get this kind of view in Los Angeles.

Bright LED flashlights shined bright in our faces. Both Zak and myself shielded our eyes with our hands.

All I could make out through my droopy eyes were shadows of two large men, what looked to be in Roman armor. Their voices sounded gruff. They were larger than normal like big and heavy weight lifters.

"What the hell!"

The startled expression made me think back to when Ozzy and the smaller guy who kidnapped us get upset when I shared with him I had a husband and kids. Could this be they saw me and realized I shouldn't be here?

Zak scooted back and kept me close.

"What the hell do you want!" His hands dropped to his sides.

My eyes had a hard time making out the men who stepped in. The light behind them was so bright. I didn't understand how Zak didn't shield his eyes.

Seeing them step in closer to our space, they dropped down a a strange long tool in their hands. They spoke to one another as if Zak and I weren't in the room. Completely ignoring his question.

"How the hell did this happen?" One man said to the other.

They paused and looked at one another, then back at Zak and I.

"I won't say anything if you won't. The other guy said as they stepped closer toward us. "You know how he hates holes in his plans."

"Why would they put a man and woman together?" The first one said.

"We are gathering the men first," said the other. "She wasn't supposed to be on this side."

My back was now pressed against the bars. There was no where else to go.

"Look, he thinks he can protect her," the first one chuckled as they inched closer toward us.

Together in sync their long weapons turned on, the static from the electricity sparked. Blue and purple veins surged up and down the weapon.

"We don't want trouble," one of them said calmly. "You both are needed—"

Zak's quick reaction punched the man talking square in the jaw and went down on the floor. The other saw and didn't react fast enough as Zak's hands were already on his chest to shove him back and try and grab his weapon.

"Liz! Run!" Zak shouted.

For that split second, the thought of leaving Zak behind put a knot in my stomach. When he yelled the second time avoiding the taser by jumping to one side, I made a run for it.

Behind me, I heard Zak cry out as the electricity struck him somewhere. The thought of him hurt after sacrificing himself to give me a fighting chance, I fought the urge not to look back.

SEPERATE WAYS

My eyes were still adjusting to the bright light. I didn't know where the hell I was running to, I had strength and the adrenaline to run free.

I jumped off the cargo train and tried to land on my feet. It was only a four foot drop and I buckled and fell as my face smacked the dirt.

My hands gripped the dirt to push myself up and sprint off the ground. I hit a brick wall of a man. There was no time to react. I bounced back straight on my butt. A bag was shoved over my head. Once again, I found myself back right where I started.

My hands were pulled behind me and zip tied. I was led by the man who was a solid rock of a human as my feet struggled to get up as I fumbled and tripped. There was no patience in him as he wanted me quickly out of whatever situation I was in.

I felt the fine dirt as my feet kicked it around with each step. I couldn't see where I was going, only the sound of feet shuffling.

Breathing heavy from the exertion and inhaling my own

bad breath, my weakened legs gave way. There was no fight in me. When he stopped and made me stand upright, the bag was pulled from my head. My eyes didn't ache as much as soft lighting was above us, high up above in two large burning torches nestled on either side of a giant wooden door. It reminded me of the appearance of a castle entrance I had seen in movies.

The starry night sky helped the adjustment of my surroundings to see a giant stone walls on either side of the door. Bewildered, I didn't know what to think or say.

Stepping toward me and blocking my view. I finally saw a clear face for the first time since my kidnapping. This man bore a shiny clean shave, big square features with short crew-cut brown hair.

The broad defined features and hard expression was anything but welcoming. I couldn't expect why I would think that, but the hard expression of a soldier stared back at me.

His brows furrowed when he saw my ring finger. He took my left hand and removed my wedding band with a strong force.

"You were not supposed to be wearing personal effects."

The gorilla grip he held made me wince in pain. Regardless, I went to snatch my ring back, but I wasn't quick enough. Panic and the heaviness in my chest caused me to try again with idiotic effort. I wasn't thinking rational. I was no match for him, he was taller, quicker and had muscles I didn't know a man of his stature could produce.

"It's okay Rebecca. It'll be okay."

I stood there confused, not sure I heard him right. Then, before I could react, he stuck me in the arm with a needle. My knees instantly buckled. I lost all of my muscle control and felt myself begin to fall. His arms wrapped around me.

"But...I'm Liz," I managed. Then I passed out.

. . .

I DREAMED Brant and I were walking along the beach on the sunny shores in Malibu. The beach was one of my favorite places to visit because of the soft sand, looking to Malibu canyon in the background with the green hills and listening to the calm shores. The water was clean, warm and the temperature always seemed to be perfect.

We walked hand in hand and I saw my two boys in front of us running bare foot and picking up rocks and throwing them into the ocean. Their laughter brought an immediate smile to my face and heart.

"This is nice." I squeezed Brant's hand. I adjusted my sunglasses, feeling the sweat building up on the bridge of my nose.

I felt the sun rays kiss my skin and spread evenly in my bikini. Brant wore nothing but his swim trunks and I noticed his stomach was more physically fit than normal.

"Since when do you work out like this?"

I touched his stomach and he gave a snicker, but it wasn't the sound of his voice. I looked up from his torso and into the eyes of what I thought Zak would look like.

I saw blue eyes soften as he stared at me. His sharp features and black hair made me lose my breath. He was tall and muscular, the image of him I'd built up in my mind, probably after he hugged me, or when I leaned on him for support.

My hand wanted to reach out and touch his torso, but I backed away. The thought scared me, I was romanticizing about him and not my husband. I felt wrong, dirty even. His skin was a perfect olive tone, with beautiful birth marks intermittently on his chest.

Zak was confused about my hesitation, gave me a bright smile and tried to reach out for me, but I stepped back further away.

"Where's Brant?" I demanded, my head turning left and right in search for him.

"You left him in Seattle, remember? This is about us now."

Something didn't feel right, yet I wasn't afraid of him. An image of being in the back of the van reappeared. My body convulsively shook.

"No!" I shouted.

I didn't want to accept what he was saying to me. He was my friend. But I wanted to know where Brant was. I know he was hear with me, I felt him, just like…my ears didn't pick up on the boys' laughter. I spun around. All three of them were gone. It was just me and Zak.

"We're stuck together. What choice do we have?" He reached out a hand to me. "I'll protect you."

The beach was fading around us. I continued to step back and whispers and whimpering were above me. *I'm asleep! I need to wake up.*

ON MY STOMACH, my head felt a few pounds heavier as my eyelids fluttered open. I could see the sun-rays shine down on the dusty stone floor. The light was bright in the room and the voices were beginning to come clear and tell others I was waking up.

My arms felt heavy as I went to push myself up. Bare feet walked by me, a cute pair of small feet with overgrown painted toe nails with green polish stopped in front of me. Her long skirt covered her feet as she knelt. She asked me in a soft muffled voice if I needed help up. She had a wooden cup with her.

The inverted triangle friendly smile glanced down on me. Her mid length light brown hair parted down the middle was loosing its curl in other areas as it had been sometime since she last combed it. Her notable broad forehead and small chin was not pointy. Her chiseled, angular cuts of the rest of her features gave her a youthful look.

She was stronger than she looked with her small frame, but she handled me well enough as the muscles in my body ached for nourishments.

She pulled me to sit on my butt and sat close for support as she put the water to my dry, cracked lips. The desperation of drinking the liquid made me gulp every drop.

"Can I get more water over here!" She said.

I was in a neatly designed stone column room that peaked like a cone. Slits of light brightened the room in almond shaped windows. My ears were starting to recognized the sounds around me. Moans, coughs and cries. I looked left and right. The room was full of women sitting up against the wall. My eyes scanned to see all the weakened fatigued spirits. Our hair was matted, makeup half on, the sadness we all wore, I wasn't the only one. There was groups of them around the room helping, like this woman was with me. My brain felt like mush and throbbed from the dehydration.

The woman who gave me water, helped me scoot closer to the edge of the wall. The sniffles and soft whimpers on either side of me made me uncomfortable. I scoot my legs closer as goosebumps formed on my body and spread with harsh, painful bumps. The chill off the stone wall felt even more uncomfortable.

Another cup of water was handed in her direction, she was kind enough to share and take my empty cup as I now sipped on my second helping. She leaned over to whisper.

"You have to wake up and clear the spot. They'll stick you."

I blinked a few times, trying to comprehend her words. My vision was still not the best, and the more I tried to look around, my vision of people blurred. I needed to focus on one image at a time. I leaned against the wall, trying to get my strength and composure under control.

I closed my eyes tight and wanted to take a deep breath, but the smell from the room lingered in my nostrils and I felt nauseous. The sour body odor drifted by. My eyes watered from the stench.

I kept my head down, trying to avoid the iron metallic smell of feminine hygiene. Or was it me? What I wanted was fresh air. This was worst than the cargo train.

Then I immediately thought about Zak. My sore eyes darted around the room and there was no sign of him, just women.

My eyes scanning to see all kinds of ethnicity. All shapes and sizes, but one thing was noticeable, we were young. Some looked very young, like their early twenties. From what I could tell, no one looked older than me.

Then, my brain registered how we all wore the same long off-white, cream-colored cotton dresses. Our sleeves were long, the neck line was at our collarbone. We all wore dresses perfectly tailored to our bodies.

Cult!

OTHER WOMEN

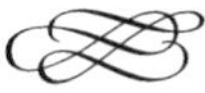

When my butt could no longer withstand the hard stone from sitting, I managed to stand. My legs felt weak, my body sore from the lack of food. Last time I had felt weak like this, I had the flu. I didn't easily get sick, but when I did, I was down for the count.

My body needed to stretch. Plus, when I breathed in from my nose, I notice the stench that drifted by was not as potent from sitting down. The room was warm from our body heat and with the sun light cascading down, I felt the rays and the heat began to increase in temperature little by little.

Mentally I was counting how many of us were in the room. *There must be at least fifty of us.*

I was given another cup of water and this time I sipped on it and thanked the woman who handed it to me. My lips tried to stretch and be pleasant, but the crack and dry skin pulled and I felt my bottom lip tear. I seethed as I continued to put my lips on the edge of the cup and allow the moisture from the water seep in.

"It's alright." The kind woman said.

Her beautiful almond shaped eyes were a tilt between in inner and outer corners. The soft color of light brown drew you into her face. In all, she was a natural beauty with light skin that had a glow that could be worn all year around.

She reminded me of a few friends back home with this natural beauty. Living in Los Angeles was hard not to think about how one could improve their appearance. From time to time I thought about the botox and lip injections to keep my youthful look as I aged. I had just turned thirty, but most women started in their early twenties. Looking at this woman, she was all natural and I hated that I compared myself to her youthful glow.

A ringing in both of my ears would not subside. I wanted to hear what other women were talking about as they kept their voices low.

The woman reached out to gently put her hand on my shoulder as she turned her figure slightly to point across the room.

"If you need the restroom, it's with the purple alexandrite stone triangle over the door."

"Why?" I didn't understand her pointing that strange fact.

The second I questioned her, my stomach dropped. A knot twisted and I felt the bile rise. My eyes widened and the woman pushed me in the direction and told me to run.

I became overwhelmed with nausea. I rushed across the room and threw open the wooden door to throw up in what looked like a wooden port-a-potty. I didn't understand where this came from. I had eaten anything in days. What was there to get rid of?

The disgusting smell of urine and feces went up in my nostrils as I cleared out and spit. My stomach felt better, but I needed to get out of the room before my body lurched to dry heave. I tried not to gag on my way out and cover my nose and mouth with my long sleeve.

I quickly closed the door behind me, pressed my back against the wall to compose myself. There was a standing sink and a mirror embedded in the wall with framed colorful jewel tones.

I washed my hands with the bar of soap and splashed water on my face. The moisture from the water was instantly refreshing. Clean hand towels were stacked neatly under the sink. As I dabbed my face, my eyes scanned up in the vintage mirror to show me my reflection was not a pretty sight.

I wore dark circles under my eyes from the worn out makeup and fatigued. My hand touched my gaunt and gray face. Most of my Southern California tan faded from lack of nourishments and sunlight.

The woman slowly came over, holding the cup in hand. A basket of used cloths were tossed after their use and I did the same.

"Thank you." I took the water and took small sips. "How did you know?"

"It was the shot they gave you. All of us had the same reaction. Over the last few days, we started to time it from when we woke up."

The woman followed me back over to our spot. The eyes of other women in the room watched me with sadness as we walked by.

"I'm Amara." She stuck her hand out. "I went to go say your name and realized we never introduced ourselves."

Shaking her firm grip, I was impressed again because her frame appeared gentle.

"Liz." I leaned against the wall and sighed. "Thank you for the warning."

"You're welcome. I was part of the first batch to arrive."

"When did you arrive?" I asked.

A part of me wanted to know if she knew how long she had been here. I couldn't have been gone for more than a few days, but then again, being trapped in the darkness with Zak, we had no sense of time.

"Oh, I believe two days. One of the Watchmen was kind to us when we arrived and shared we needed to throw up in the bathroom because of the shot." Amara chatted with me like we were old friends.

We slumped down on the wall side by side. Her peppy attitude was a bit hard for me to adjust to. I could see she needed to talk with someone and obviously in the room had their own clicks.

"Most of us didn't make it to the restroom on the first day." Amara's voice quieted and she leaned over to me. "One Watchmen in particular wasn't happy about the mess and made us clean it up. He was nasty to us and when you see him, you can tell he isn't right."

Comprehending my situation, seeing the women and now learning names. I felt like I was stuck in a strange Twilight Zone moment.

"Watchmen? Who are they?" I asked.

The name sounded silly to me. Like a Game of Thrones reference I didn't understand.

Being off my feet helped my stomach settle. I sipped the water, looking into the cup, I could see I was running low. The sink was across the room and the thought of getting back up on my feet mentally exhausted me.

Amara began to play with her finger in the dirt, drawing spirals.

"They are the guards. They follow orders, but we haven't seen from who. The mean Watchman stood over us with his long electric taser to poke and taunt us."

The sudden change in her demeanor was now timid. Her eyes focused on her drawings of spirals in the dirt.

"A few women have fought back. We watched at they were tased, harassed and thrown into the locker."

She looked into my eyes when I did not speak and probably saw the million questions burning in my brain but I didn't know where to start or what to ask.

"I overheard a Watchman mention that your batch was the last to arrive. There should be sixty of us now." She said.

My mouth dropped. "Sixty! For what? Do you know why we are here?"

She shrugged her shoulders. "One day I was lying on a tropical beach and the next thing I knew, I was in the back of a van with no sound to the outside world with another woman, tied up and scared."

"It's a Government thing." One woman said to my left.

"No, it's a cult." Another woman said to my right.

The other women in the room began to chime in their theories. I was listening to that it was a billionaires club sacrifice and we would all be killed. To it was the Illuminati and we were going to be brain washed. What this told me, no one knew anything.

This made the voices in the room rise with frustration and everyone thought in their own way they had it right. The voices and shrieks was a lot to handle.

"Alright!" Amara shouted. "Alright! We could do this all day and night. Let's remember to stick together and don't give those Watchmen a reason to come back in here."

When she said the name, Watchmen. The women pressed their lips together and there was hushes and stopped. The room was quiet again, the fear in the women's eyes who have experienced the Watchmen were teary, wide and shook.

Amara wiped her spirals and circles on the floor. She didn't want anyone else to see it and her legs stretched out over the area.

"When she comes back, we can ask her if she overheard anything. That's...when she comes back."

Taken a back, I nearly forgot what we were talking about. "Who? When?"

Amara leaned over to me to whisper.

"My travel companion, Nelli. She fought back and was defiant, so they took her to the locker."

"The locker?"

"Someplace where they take those who will not cooperate. She's been there for almost two days now. Can't say I don't blame her for not adapting to…whatever this is."

The sound of metal unlocking startled me. Other women scrambled, worried as they rushed to stand up and have their backs to the wall.

Amara quickly got to her feet and helped me up to mine.

"Just do as I do." She warned.

WATCHMEN

On the opposite side of the room, large almond red cedar doors with blacked iron bolts and hinges were automatically opening. Slowly the doors opened inward. The dust from the bottom floor sifted in the direction as the doors opened all the way and to rest and echo as it stopped against the walls.

Men lined up in a straight line across the entrance. Their tall physique chics were in the shadows of what I could see was a hallway. My eyes counted ten men. At their sides were long sticks they held in one hand.

Amara leaned over. "Watchmen."

Her soft whisper could barely be heard, but definitely loud enough for me to recognized and swallow the lump in my throat.

The entrance was long enough for them to walk in unison as they entered the room. Each Watchmen in size was intimidating as their stature well over six feet in height and large and muscular physiques. It reminded me of the Professional Wrestlers Brant and the boys watched a few times a week. I called it a men's soap opera because it had trash talk, beautiful women and big muscular men wrestling and diving off of extreme heights during a match.

Their Neanderthal facial structures were hard to read. I was always sensitive to other people's energy. How they marched into the room, no word from their lips, and carrying hard expressions.

The other women found their immediate presence threatening. When one of the long tasers was switched on, I felt the energy of women around me shiver and try not to whimper. My palms rested against the wall. Both of my shoulders were being pushed in from the other women growing tighter together.

My eyes scanned each one of them. I wanted to remember their faces and in truth, I didn't know if any one of them could be Zak. Their eyes were all different shades. Some had facial hair and beards and others clean shaven. Their hair was short or long and in buns.

Their armor was a medieval bronzed chest piece and leather straps with a belt around them. They looked authentic, from a different time. Their short cotton sleeved shirts underneath were perfectly tailored to sculpt their figures.

In the center of the line, my eyes stopped at the squared face clean shaven, wide piercing baby blue eyes. For a split second, I thought the man was Ozzy. My heart stopped, but this man was smaller at the shoulders, his ears folded out at the tips almost to a point and his lips smaller. His dark brows furrowed staring back at me. This man's eyes were the type of cold that when he looked at you, it was like he was looking into your soul.

We locked eyes, his head tilted not wavering from mine. He stepped forward as the other men stood still and he made his way over to me.

The dark hair curled at his ears. The sharp features on his

face gave me a sly smile with his thin lips than ran chills up my spine. The paleness of his skin reminded me of someone who lived in snow and didn't see much light. Those eyes watched me, like I was a piece of meat.

As he grew closer, I could see the pressed dark bronze protective chest piece of the giving tree. The leather flaps from his belt, slapped on his thighs with each step. My breathing so shallow, I nearly forgotten how to breathe.

When he came closer, the women spread far apart from us like a virus. My back to the wall, I wished at this moment I could melt into the wall and break away from his eerie site on me.

His feet stopped half a foot away from me. Slowly he raised his weapon to have the electronic pulse warm my face. It sparked, and I jumped. He lips slightly curved. The spark in his eye was joy as he got off on fear. The nerves in my body produced a bile in my throat I swallowed to keep down.

He leaned in closer, inches from my face as his weapon illuminated the pale blue in his eyes to nearly a white. I was frightened and shaking. With one click, his weapon turned off. I sucked up a sharp breath. Afraid to move, but relieved the weapon wasn't going to be used on me.

Our gaze didn't break. When he spoke, my spine tensed as he projected to everyone in the room.

"I see the fear in all of your eyes," he said. "You do not fool me. Many women have tried, and they have ended up in the locker, is that what you want?"

With a sharp turn, he broke our gaze and began to pace the room. Looking into the eyes of every other woman. Terrified to say anything, besides his projected voice, the silence in the room built up a negative energy that I felt flow each of us as we pressed against each other and the wall so tightly, it made it hard to breathe.

"Sixty of you have been carefully chosen to be here." He said.

His feet shuffled on the floor as he rushed back over to me and put his weapon under my chin and lifted my head for my eyes to meet his. All he had to do was flip it as his thumb rested on the on button on the handle. If he chose to, I would get the shock of my life. My hands were clammy against the wall. Sweat ran down my back.

The gasps from other women made a few whimpers around us. I was terrified inside, I could feel my body shake uncontrollably as my legs were already tired and still sore from dehydration. I saw the glint in his eyes, he wanted to flip the switch and see what would happen. When he lingered for a few more seconds, the weapon dropped and the pressure from my chin felt the immediate relief.

"You have all been selected to be here. You should be honored."

He continued to pace the other side of the room. His tone was a suggestion we should even be thankful to be in his presence. Amara gently took my hand and squeezed.

"Ladies, your rebirth will begin tomorrow," the man announced. "I would like to suggest you all behave, stay calm and reclaim your womanhood by the gifts you will bare fruit for."

The large metal clank from the heavy doors slowly began to move back and close. One by one the Watchmen turned and left the room as they marched in unison. He was the last one to leave, stepping backward on his way out looking at all of us. It was when he broke the hard expression for the evil smile reminded me of someone cold and calculated. He was going to hurt one or many of us. I could feel it deep within my bones. He was the threat and probably the one in charge of this nonsense.

The doors closed, the lock sealed through the metal grates. Everyone breathed a sigh of relief. I leaned over, putting my hands on my knees to take in deep breaths from the terror of that man.

SILVER WOLF

My boys were laughing and playing in the backyard. We had a trampoline at home and watching them bounce with their acrobatic tricks was the best part about my days with them.

Constantly the boys shouted for me to watch them, when my eyes never left them in the first place.

"You got this, Steven." I encouraged as I clapped.

I could still remember the background with my green grass, built-in smoker, pool, rockslide and palm trees surrounding the area.

I was interrupted by Amara's voice in the background. I turned around to see her in my house, standing at my sliding glass door asking me to come in. In my dream, I even knew it didn't feel right to see her. Amara waved at me to come inside.

The laughter of my boys' voice stopped. My head turned to see them. The trampoline was stiff. Dark clouds rolled in to cover the blue sky. There was no life in my backyard. The water from the rockslide stopped, my palm trees dried and brittle and so was my grass. An emptiness suddenly consumed my heart.

Amara's voice continued to call for me as if nothing was wrong. The thumping of my heart was ready to burst out of my chest. The fear poured on me like frozen water. My feet planted on the ground. My kitchen window had the vines of my faux ivy leaves began to grow around the window and Amara was getting consumed by the growth. The shattering of my windows as the vines grew out and onto the house, broke my doors, and regardless, Amara still stood without a care still smiling back at me.

I COUGHED, inhaling the dust from the floor. The stone was cold on my face and body. Amara handed me her companion's blanket since she was in the locker and had no need of it.

"Use it as a pillow." Amara suggested.

Most of the women were sleeping. It was the middle of the night and the darkness had crept in, but the almond shaped slits allowed the bright full moon to cascade its light faintly.

My body rose up and I wrapped the blanket around my shoulders as my arms wrapped around my legs. I heard Amara's soft snore next to me and it brought a slight joy to my ears. I was taking in my new predicament and trying to understand what this all meant. Why us?

My mind began to race as my ears listened to the snores, the tossing and turning of others. The whimpers as I could see some women cried in their sleep. My dream had shaken me, felt too real and I needed to occupy my mind on something else.

It terrified me there were no answers to this place. We were sitting ducks in this room and the fear of how I was stripped of everything and from everyone. The thought of fighting to stay alive was a dangerous game of Russian Roulette.

How we were all stuck in this room, dressed the same. They wanted us to mentally break, be coerced and trust them. As a teacher, there are many training classes we have to attend and this was one of the signs of what was being done to us.

The malnutrition, weak capabilities and the dependency on who would be in charge. Even in my exhausted brain, all I could think of that this was some type of cult. What was scary to think, they kidnapped their followers, when normally you are the follower looking for redemption, or a new way to live, or born into it and don't know the difference.

All of us that I was aware of weren't either. We had no clear understanding why we were chosen, what made us special? Usually cults are a choice, this felt more like a prison sentence.

My eyelids fluttered as I was half asleep and deep in thought. My heart ached at the thought to easily close my eyes and slip into a dream. I wanted nothing more to see Brant and the boys. When I did, I could sense I was at peace. Then waking up back into my reality made me scared and anxious all over again.

I thought about Zak and already missed him. I wondered if he was in a room like me somewhere, but with men, or was he taken somewhere else? Mentally, I was still beating myself up for giving up when I jumped from the train car. I should have ran faster and fought harder. I should have pushed myself further. I should have fought harder for my freedom.

My hand went to feel for my wedding ring and band. The pain in my chest grew to a heartache as my last precious one carat diamond was all that I had left, and now it was gone. It was hard to digest my rings were no longer on my finger. Just the reminder of the indentation that it was once there.

The howling of a wolf outside perked my ears. I quietly stood on my feet and walked over to one of the windows where I thought the sound could come from. My hand rested against the cold stone and there was the beauty in a silver wolf standing on a slope in the distance in the middle of a field and howling. How I envied that animal's freedom.

"Is it beautiful?"

A soft feminine voice in an Aerobic accent startled me on my right. Surprised to see beautiful big dark brown exotic eyes stare back at me. Her shorter face and small forehead made her look childlike. Her big brown eyes and pouty lips smiles back at me as her natural, long think black hair was tied in a braid at one side and draped over her shoulder.

I nodded. "I hope I didn't wake you."

She shook her head and whispered she had a hard time sleeping herself. As my eyes drifted back to see the wolf in all his glory, it had already left and was not in view any longer. I sighed, disappointed as I felt that animal too had abandoned me.

"It's gone." My voice couldn't hide the sadness. The woman stayed by me, she probably needed to talk. "How are you with all of this?"

"Trying to keep it together for myself and my sister," she said with a faint accent coming through.

My eyes widened at the shock she and her sister were taken. "Your family has to be beside themselves knowing both their daughters are gone."

She shrugged her shoulders. "We have never known our parents." She paused before she continued and put out her hand. "I'm Yasmin."

I shook her firm grip. "Liz. So, do you have family?"

Yasmin shook her head. "We escaped our country about

ten years ago and came to America. It's just been the two of us. We have friends, but more like what you call…acquaintances."

"I see," I said. "I'm sorry that you both have to be here, but at least you have each other."

Yasmin smiled. "Very true. What do you think this is about?"

Looking down at my gown, I snagged at it from my waist.

"Other than matching dresses, I would say we are forced to be here." Using the words made my mouth dry. Saying this out loud made me feel uneasy. "A part of some type of cult is my thought." The goosebumps spread evenly up my arms and neck. I shuddered at the thought.

There was a whimper in the distance. Yasmin turned to see her sister have some sort of nightmare. She excused herself to go and help settle her sister back to sleep. I made my way back over to my spot. I settled next to Amara and laid down. I couldn't even recall the moment I drifted off to sleep.

AMARA SHOOK MY SHOULDER GENTLY, talking to me that it was time to get up. A wooden bowl was in her hands. She was offering me fresh fruit.

The sweet smell of cantaloupe, honey dew, and pineapple made my mouth salivate. As my body rose from the floor, the line of women standing quietly in the hallway were served bowls of fruit for breakfast.

I moved back toward the end of the line. Many of the women standing in their groups, eating with their fingers as the joy on their faces spread and changed their attitudes. The energy in the room was less agitation.

My face felt gritty as I rubbed my eyes. I so badly wanted and desperately needed a shower. My hair was greasy and I was jealous at those who could tie their hair into a bun with no tie. My hair was too thick for that.

When my eyes glanced down, the dust covered my gown. My hands gently tried to wipe what dust I could off, without creating a choking hazard. I wanted just enough off me where I didn't look completely homeless, even though I just realized in a way, I was.

When I approached the table, one woman was handing out the bowls with a warm smile. Her silver to nearly white hair was shiny and perfectly styled in a braid that was long toward the waist and worn on one shoulder. Her beautiful milk, smooth skin was breathtaking to see in person. Her oval face and wide cheek bones didn't give her sharp or angular curves. Her forehead and jawline are slightly smaller as the edges of her face are rounded.

Her nose was smaller at the bridge, but stood out when she turned to one side reaching back for a bowl from her helper, that was dressed down in a brown top wrapped at her waist with a matching skirt. She had an apron on and the helper wore a bonnet that tied at the back of her head and kept her red hair from poking out.

The helper had one job. She was to pour fruit contents into the bowl, hand it to the silver-haired woman and then do it again. She looked miserable doing it, like she would rather be somewhere else.

Same!

When a bowl was filled, the silver-haired woman went to grab it as her full lips stretched in a smile when seeing me. Her big, prominent green cat eyes with long lashes stared back at me.

"Here you are." The silver-haired woman went to hand me a wooden bowl.

The woman helping her snatched the bowl back. She was short, frumpy, and sour faced. The rounded features, plump cheeks and small mouth was a bitter soul. Compared to the rest of us women, these two looked freshly washed in clean clothing.

"She's already been up here!" She kept the bowl back to her waist, denying the silver-haired woman.

My stomach growled, just a foot away from real food. Appalled how the frumpy woman didn't seem to care for me, for no good reason as her face soured.

"I have not!" I snapped back.

The silver-haired woman was in a state of shock at both of us. She was in the middle, took another look at me and shook her head.

"I don't remember her, please hand me the bowl." Her hand out in gesture.

The frumpy woman held back the bowl. "No. She got her serving. Wench wants to sneak more."

"Wench?" My disgust in her tone. "What are you, from the 1600s?"

The frumpy women dumped my fruit contents back into the serving bowl. There was so much fruit, we could have had a third helping if we were granted.

The silver-haired woman, annoyed, stood and snatched up another bowl.

"You're dismissed." She hissed at the frumpy woman.

When there was about to be a protest. The silver-haired woman held up her hand.

"Here."

The silver-haired woman handed me the bowl. Taking a good look at her, she couldn't have been that much older than me. With her beautiful braided hair draped to one side, she clasped her hands as she stood.

The lavish long yellow gown with forest green stitched threads of vines along the border of the dress and sleeves made me feel more disgusting than I already felt. I naturally looked down to compare myself to her.

The gown reminded me of the Renaissance. As the silk shimmered in the streaks of light from behind her. She made her way around the table.

My greedy, dirty fingers picked up the honey dew first and shoved it in my mouth. The sweet burst of the melon on my tongue and the juices slid down my throat was a satisfaction of hunger I promised never to take for granted again.

When my eyes looked up to the silver-haired woman watching me eat. My cheeks flushed. "I haven't eaten in days." My voice croaked.

Her lips stretched across her face. When she came from around the table, she looked at me with her hands clasped at her stomach as the heel of her shoes echoed in the room.

"You must be part of the last batch, welcome." The warmth in her tone gave me the wrong set of vibes because I didn't want to be welcomed. I wanted to be home.

DINING HALL

After breakfast, the Watchmen came to have us line up and follow them to the end of the hallway. I didn't see the one with the cold eyes and I was thankful, because I had a feeling, my encounters with him were going to be fueled by trouble. In the best line formation we could achieve, Amara and I stayed toward the back, wanting to be as dead last as possible. If I watched from the end of the line, this gave me the opportunity to scope things out. Stay out of view from the people that seemed to have some control or run this place.

The long and narrow hallway continued the architecture of stone, candle lit walls, tapestry hanging and stained colored glass for windows. The gothic style windows were few and far between. I managed to pass by one with stone seating as the depth of the window stuck out.

This place keeps getting interesting.

As we walked down, we were entering into another room. Whispers among the ones toward the front mentioned that we were going into the dining hall.

There was a Watchman every sixth window standing

guard. Ready to put us back in line if necessary. The silly thought went through my brain. Looking up at the ceiling and taking notice of the cameras placed within the walls, someone was always keeping an eye on us.

The line moved swiftly. All of us were quiet, too afraid to disrupt or cause a scene. The man with the cold blue eyes stood at the entrance, watching us enter. He enjoyed giving each of the women an uncomfortable stare.

We made eye contact for a few seconds and he gave me a devilish smile that made me shiver. I didn't want trouble, my eyes dropped, but he still managed to hold up the line and stop me at the entrance with his taser weapon.

"Good morning," he said to me.

"Morning."

I made it sharp and quick. My eyes stayed to the ground. He leaned close to my ear.

"You look lonely. I could have you pay me a visit later."

I bit my bottom lip to keep it from quivering and show any signs of weakness to him. My knees wanted to buckle. My hands clenched into fists and waited for the moment he grew tired of me and allowed me to pass by.

When he touched the wood post in the middle between the two doors. Me and a few females jumped back. He grabbed me by the arm and yanked me close to him.

"You don't need to be afraid of me."

His lips and hot breath were inches from my neck. I wanted to crawl out of my skin and die at this point. This man was going to make my life miserable.

"Hunter, what is the hold up?" said another male voice from the other side of the hallway.

"Just lost their footing is all."

He stared at me and let me go to continue my walk into the dining hall.

Leaving his pretense was a terrifying and yet subtle relief.

His strong energy was a form of evil. *Hunter was his name?* His name was grimly fitting. He stalked me like I was his prey.

Amara put a hand on my back. "You ok?"

I nodded. I didn't need to draw anymore attention to myself.

The ceiling arched like a cylinder. The smooth stone work from floor to ceiling was impressive. Large long stained mirrored glass windows resembled a nature scene with a bear one side catching a fish in a river, and the other resembled a stag fighting the bear in a battle on a hill.

We all sat close together on the benches at the table, all of us facing in the direction north of the room. There was a small stage with a large table and two thrones made of dark carved cherry wood and purple satin for the cushion. The satin also had hand stitched decorations, but I was too far back to make out what it was.

The room was brighter than any other room I had been in so far. My neck ached and I could feel the migraine form in the back of my skull from the stress of my morning. Taking all of this in was hard each day. The unknown was consuming me into madness. A man like Hunter around had me pegged as his toy to play and mentally torture with.

Amara nudged me to sit up straight. Some of the Watchmen took notice. The last thing she must have wanted was for me to get in trouble. When I sat up, I couldn't help and follow her gaze as one Watchmen wore a different chest piece that had silver melted on the front of the tree of life. Her cheeks flushed watching him.

It took me a moment, but I remembered him as the man I first saw when I arrived. The big muscular military guy. He was against the wall keeping guard and I caught him looking at Amara. He didn't give me the uncomfortable vibe, like Hunter.

I leaned over to Amara. "You have an admirer."

She followed my eyes in his direction and he shifted uncomfortably because he had been caught, and cleared his throat.

My eyes drifted up to an the elegant looking silver haired woman. She passed by us walking down the middle of the isle in graceful and calculated steps as her heels continued to echo in the large hall. Her hands clasped at the bottom of her stomach. She was all grace.

She took center stage and waited for the last few women to sit. The uneasy sound of the doors to the room closing echoed in the room.

"Young ladies!"

She didn't need to project her voice. There was a small microphone somewhere on her clothing. The surround sound in the room was hidden in the walls.

"Welcome," she said. "You all have arrived in your new home. Many of you traveled far..."

She paused as we all looked at one another as if to concur. A few tables ahead of me, someone rose from their seat. She was tall, gangly looking with short blonde hair.

"Booooooo!" The anger and linger to stretch out the heckle.

The gangly woman looked around the crowd and wanted more to participate with her reaction, but everyone else including myself was scared to death to breathe loudly let alone boo someone on stage.

"This is not necessary." The silver-haired woman kindly rejected.

"Boooooo! This is crap! You rich people and your demented ways! Just kill us and get it over with!"

A swift hand from the silver-haired woman rose, the Watchmen in immediate reaction to the gangly woman stopped in command, ready to draw their weapons.

"No! Let me handle this," said the silver-haired woman.

"Handle what?" The gangly woman looked around. "You kidnapped us, ripped us from our homes, starved us and you want us to sit here and listen to you?"

Other women in the audience began to agree with nodding and speaking up.

"Enough!" The Military Watchmen raised his voice in a boom, it felt like my father yelling at me and made me shiver.

"Just take her to the locker." Hunter was eager for the excitement as his thumb turned his weapon on.

The sudden cries and pleas from women stirred the room. They began to scoot away as the gangly woman stood her ground.

When the silver-haired woman nodded at a few Watchman on the opposite side, they marched over. Both had their weapon on and one of them stuck the gangly woman in the stomach like a jab of a knife. In horror, she went down like a sack of rocks. Then, she was dragged out of the room. This was setting the precedence about speaking and stepping out of line.

The silver haired woman remained calm, nothing phased her.

"Ladies that chose to speak out of turn or over me," she said, "shall be put in the locker."

She scanned the room, waiting for anyone else to speak up. No one did.

HIS GRACE

"For the next three months you will learn the fundamentals of your new life," the silver-haired woman said. "You will carry out chores and help restore and rebuild what our Grace has envisioned for us."

The silver haired woman's enthusiasm and passion for her mission was annoying to me. She bowed and stayed in position. The odd behavior I witness was a terrible act of a play.

Everyone jumped to the sound of trumpets from the surround sound of a welcoming reception.

"You've got to be joking."

I put my hand over my heart, feeling the hard thud in my chest. *This has to be some sort of sick joke? This can't be real!*

I was waiting for the camera crew to be shown and all of this was an act. A very elaborate act, but this behavior was nuts!

The dining hall doors automatically opened and we were asked to rise to our feet. My five-foot-four did me no favors as a good portion of the woman around me were over five-six. A man walked down the aisle and nodded to some woman as he made his way to the stage.

He was tall, thin in frame, with dirty blond hair to his shoulders, and I couldn't believe it, but this weirdo wore a gold crown on his straight haired head. There looked to be a shadow of a matching beard, from what I could see.

Once he got to the front on stage. I wasn't able to see much until we were asked to take a seat.

The man that wore the crown kissed the top of the silver-haired woman's head, and asked us to applaud in her honor for a warm introduction. We did so ever lightly, confused now more than ever.

When he sat on what I would assume was his throne, the silver-haired woman took the throne to his right and they sat together.

I pressed my lips together, keeping in the laughter that was building in my chest. He too wore a Renaissance attire with his black velvet wardrobe and gold embroidered thread. The jewels on his crown were a vibrant emerald. The top of the crown was carefully crafted and molded into thorn branches.

I must have fallen into a coma and this must be all a dream.

I was praying at this point and wishing beyond all hope this was my answer. This man sitting in is throne resembled a younger version of a famous King I couldn't but my finger on it. The thick black velvet robes puffed from the shoulders and elbows. His square face bore the face of boredom. His forehead, cheekbones and jaw looked to be equal as the edges of his face were angular and his chin a bit flatter. His lips straight and thin.

As the music slowly softened, we all waited for something to be said. His sunken small eyes glanced around at us and his thumb and forefinger rubbed back and forth against his neatly trimmed beard. The other hand tucked his shoulder length blonde hair behind one ear.

"First order of business." His annoyed tone was precise. "When your Grace walks into the room, you shall rise and when your Grace sits, you sit ... Let's try this again."

He stood from his table and like me and everyone else in the room, we rose. He stared into the crowd for a few seconds. When he sat, we did the same.

There were a few stragglers in the crowd and he shared it was a learning curve and we should have it down by the end of the week. When everyone in the crowd rose and sat in unison, he was pleased with a sly grin, which made my stomach turn.

You have control over us, good for you, you prick!

His hands rested as he gripped the arms of his chair. "You all have been through a terrible ordeal. Mother..." He gestured to the silver-haired woman on his right, "and I want to make this transition as easy as possible. We will give you answers..."

One woman went to speak as she slowly rose to her feet, raising her hand. His Grace put a hand up to stop her.

"Speaking about your Grace, or over, or interrupt is forbidden. It's an immediate dismissal into the locker, understood?"

All of us kept quiet. To me his watchful eyes took in our behavior. He observed, seeming like a hard man to please. His Watchmen were intimidating with hard expressions, height and build. His Grace reminded me of someone very cold and calculated. What was scary, he didn't show his emotions because he probably had sinister intentions.

"Understand this," he said then. "Your lives before your journey are considered your past lives. They are a memory, but not a place you will return to, ever."

Other women and including myself gasped. His Grace waited a few seconds to allow us to digest this information.

"Your only way out of here is death."

A woman burst into tears as she covered her face. A few women behind me sniffed their runny noses. My eyes watered as the fear draped over me like a thick blanket. A burden to weigh heavily over my mental stability.

When he rose from his seat, we slowly and bitterly obeyed and he smiled in satisfaction.

"Wonderful, ladies. I want you to understand, this new life is revolutionary," he started. "Yes, there are sacrifices to be made, new orders to obey and live by, but I promise you, you are all better off. Mother will help you all through this journey with careers and classes. You will treat her with the upmost respect."

"I am your Grace. You will all address me as such. I am your ruler, the man to follow into your new life."

The boots of his heels clicked on the stage as he slowly made his way to the stairs. The sound of each step was like a hammer to a nail as I felt my fate was being nailed shut in my coffin.

"You are all here because you were chosen to be here. It was not random pickings, this was designed for you."

I could feel my pulse quicken in my neck. My blood pressure was rising, I could feel the warmth in my cheeks as I bit down bitterly.

My eyes watched for the Watchmen and their weapons. I didn't want to be stuck by those.

How could he think he was going to get away with this? It was the annoying sound in his tone, as though we should believe in his words, and be thankful to be in his presence.

His Grace continued stepping down the stairs and pace in the aisles. He appeared to try and be on our level, thinking he could help us understand. Watchmen followed and stood close to make sure no one made any sudden moves.

"Your family is everyone in this room. Take a look around, we have each other."

He paused and wanted everyone to take a look around with his hand gesture from left to right. When we did, it pleased him.

"We shall build on this land. We will prosper and create new families. It is simple, really. The road to get you all here was difficult, but now you will all flourish."

As he made his rounds in his speech and made it back on stage, he gestured with open arms there was more to share.

"Young ladies, I welcome you home to Silver Pines."

His Grace was ready to walk off stage and the blaring of the trumpets from the speakers made all of us jump. When his Grace walked passed, nodding and giving his hand to a few women who were already a fan of his, I wanted to be sick.

Why couldn't I wake from this dream?

As the Watchman walked close to his Grace to make sure no one else got out of hand, he was nearly as tall as his own Watchmen. He was slimmer, shoulders were shorter and his clothing hid a good portion of what his frame could be.

"He serious?" I couldn't help myself and speak out loud.

"How the hell were we picked?" Amara was just as skeptical as I was.

THE WOMEN'S TOWER

"Alright ladies," Mother said. "Back to the women's tower."

As we left, we formed a line, she was pleased with our ability to follow instructions. I want to roll my eyes, but I was careful because I could sense there were many hidden cameras in this place and I wasn't sure if it was their mission to catch us in the act.

A part of me wanted to run as fast as I could and find a way out of this place.

Be smart about this.

In order to survive, I must bury deep down those urges of speaking my mind, being defiant, or difficult. What I really needed to concentrate on, was study this place, to plan my escape.

"Silver Pines." Amara was amused by the name. "I wonder if it means something?"

"Better yet, where the heck do you think we are?" I leaned back to answer her as we walked.

Walking down the long stone hallway, the cleanliness of the new build of this solid foundation was not missed. Seeing out the slits of the windows, I could barely see another side of this place off in the distance. If there are sixty women, was there an equal amount of men? Did all the men become Watchmen? I wondered what Zak was going through. Was he alright? In the locker?

The terrible waft of lingering body odor from the women's tower struck our nostrils as we entered the room. None of us had combed our hair, brushed our teeth, or were given a spray or dry stick to help mask our hormonal scent.

Someone turned around to Mother.

"Aint we gonna get a shower soon? I'm tired of smelling all these damn coochies."

The woman put her hands on her hips as we walked by. I put my fingers to my lips to withhold the laugh that was ready to burst from my chest.

Mother's eyebrows raised and was not amused. "You will speak to me with respect and a gentler tone."

"We could get sick from disease you know." The woman crossed her arms over her large chest.

Mother stood still. Her serious expression did not back down.

"Need I remind you?"

The woman brushed off Mother and under her breath she mumbled words I couldn't understand, but could imagine it wasn't pleasantries.

Naturally like human instinct. We all had our areas and went back to them. I slid down the wall and sat on my butt as Amara sat Indian style across from me. Her big light brown eyes indicated she wanted to talk, I didn't blame her. What else could we do to pass the time?

"WAIT, YOUR TRAVEL COMPANION WAS A MAN?" Amara couldn't help but say it again in shock.

A woman who continued to be on her own walked around the room and lightly touched her finger tips to the wall. She walked in between us and her body odor made us want to gag. No one said anything but cover their noses when she came by. She continued to walk in the circular tower for hours. Again, What was she to do to pass the time? I didn't blame her, but felt bad no one tried to be friend her.

"What was his name?" Amara asked and made me snap back into our conversation.

"Zak." I continued to worry about him. "He was very kind and protective."

"Did you ever get to see what he looked like?" Amara's wide eyed curiosity made me smile.

"No." I shook my head. "Not clearly. I imagined seeing his outline in the darkness."

"And? What did you imagine?" Amara's chin rested on her hands.

"Tall and seemed fit. Maybe a gym rat type of guy. He ate healthy, he shared his power bar with me in the beginning. Dark hair and for some reason I picture blue eyes."

Amara sighed as she imagined the thought of what Zak could look like. Brining him up and how I described him didn't feel right. I had been worried about him, but I shouldn't. He was a complete stranger and yes, he listened to me and tried to help me escape, but I felt I was painting the wrong image.

"Anyways, It was only for a short period of time." I said.

Amara straightened up at the change of my tune. Her lips parted, ready to say something, but someone else interjected before her.Two other women overheard our conversation and gravitated toward us.

"You were bunked with a man?"

Yasmin and her identical twin sister came over. My eyes were stunned to see two people as one, it had been sometime since I had seen a pair of identical twins up close. Their difference was their eye color. Yasmin's were big and brown and her sister, she introduced to us as Esther, her eyes were hazel.

If you didn't catch the eye color, sitting down was hard to truly determine their difference. They were thinned framed with no bust or butt. Yet, I could sense Yasmin was the twin who took pride in her appearance as she sat upright, and shoulders back, her hair still in the braid that rested on her shoulder.

Esther slumped on the ground and even with their untidy hair, her hair was turning into a birds nest it was so frizzy.

As they introduced themselves, I learned Yasmin was the oldest of the pair. Her voice had a slight twitch of a higher octave. She could imitate her sister right on cue, where Esther had a more difficult time.

They were both interested to hear what I had to say about my kidnapping, my husband, and my male companion. More women during the course of the night flocked to listen to my stories about my children and how Brant saved for our trip.

After a while, I took notice I was the center of attention to most of the women in the room. It reminded me of Summer camp when my sister and I went as kids. At nights, the camp counselors made us sit around the fire pit in a circle, as we ate s'mores and told ghost stories.

Shannon was always a better story teller. She was animated and knew the timing of when to make people jump. I sat, so intrigued by the tales, I was the one emerged with my hands ready to cover my eyes at a scene that was too scary to handle, even when nothing was there.

Now, I was the center of attention. I was used to this being a school teacher, but it was easier to talk to elementary kids about scholastics. Talking about my life, I tended to shy away from. I didn't want to know people about me, because I would feel their pity or judging eyes.

Back home, whenever I told my story about Brant and the boys were my step-sons, I always got the question. Are you and Brant having kids?" When I would shake my head, I got the eye roll from women it was because I didn't want to fully commit, or I didn't like kids.

I have learned if I share it was because of my uterus problems. That's when the pity set in, I got the tilted heads, sad eyes, and the hand on the shoulder. The same words came out of their mouthes, sharing what a wonderful person I was to Brant and the boys, and how I should be so lucky that I am with someone who could make me a mother.

It was hard to digest when they went from judging me one minute, and trying to make me sound selfish I didn't want children, to the fake sympathy and support if I shared my fertility issues.

Now, I sat in a room full of women who were complete strangers listening to my story of how I got here. I didn't have to explain myself like before, because they didn't know me. They took me for my word I was a mother of two boys. For once in my life, sharing in a group felt calming and reassuring that what I had outside these walls, was worth fighting for.

In the night more women would share a story with the rest of us. Like a teacher on the first day of school. I wanted everyone to say their first name, where they were from and how old they were before they could share a story about themselves.

My ears picked up on the different accents from the south, East and West Coast. Other women like the twins were not from this country and I heard a few asian dialects and one Canadian accent. In their stories, I was picking up on, how I was the only one in the room married with kids.

So far, we were all ranging from twenty-two to me being the oldest at thirty. A wide vast of education or skillsets like farming, sewing and basic life careers.

In my training skills, there were key elements to follow when listening to someone's story. How they introduce themselves. Are they confident in their story telling? Did they mention family? Is family important, or was it friends? Their intellectual grammar choices when describing themselves was important.

Just like children, I evaluated each one that shared. In my mind I was tallying how many awkward, or disassociated introvert personas. These women were outcasts. No one else seemed to share family stories, or they didn't have family. Most of them came from a hard life.

Other women were picking up the same information and drawing their own conclusions. I felt different, being married with children and then I was the only female so far in the room when I was kidnapped. My journey was shared with Zak, while the rest of them had each other.

WE WERE all startled in the morning as the iron bar on the door unlatched and the doors slowly opened. Scattered and rushing around, we stood to our feet as quickly as we could. If anything was to get anyone going, it was waking up in a panic. Disoriented as I stood with my back against the wall, I was irritated smelling not only my body odor, but other's as we stood close, our shoulders touched. At this point, I thought I would be used to it, but it seemed another morning of feminine hygiene at its ripest time.

In a line outside the door. Only one Watchmen walked into our room. It was the one I first saw, recalling how he called me Rebecca before he injected me. The one Amara seemed to have eyes for. My head tilted in her direction and the flush in her cheeks, watching him intently spread up her neck and face.

He carried himself with a calm, yet timid walk. He looked above us, not at us.

Taking a closer look. I hadn't noticed the two bears on either side of the tree of life. The bears were on their hind legs with their claws out. A crown above the tree, like his Grace wore was above in a resemblance of power. The emblem was forged into their chest pieces.

He was direct like a soldier, with perfect form when he walked, but he wasn't a man to fear, not like Hunter.

"Ladies." Before he continued, he pulled his weapon from his belt and set it on the ground. "Do not be afraid. I kindly ask you come off the wall and don't feel I am a threat to you."

When most of the women hesitated, he turned to talk to his men.

"Close the door." He ordered to them.

There was confusion all around. One of the Watchmen went to question, but with a sharp glance back. He nodded and then pressed on the side wall to have the doors close.

He turned back and continued. "Ladies, I want to introduce myself as a Commander of the Watchmen," he said. "My name is Reynard. We are here to protect you and to serve his Grace."

Hands behind his back, he stood tall and proud in a firm stance his legs only a foot apart.

"Our community believes in his Grace. You are all here for a reason. A reason within time will be explained to you."

I caught myself staring at his rectangle face. His high forehead and angular edges was quite symmetrical. His jaw was a squared-off shape with long features to match. He was a big human being, almost unnatural as it appeared monotonous.

"The Watchmen are here for protection. They are here to

make sure law and order go hand in hand. Others outside these walls will teach you the ways. Listen to them, learn from them. Making his Grace happy means privileges."

The instant delivery of his words, my gut believed. There was something in his authoritative voice that drew me in. Including myself, other women didn't have their guard up as much. Reynard's shoulders relaxed a bit. The energy in the room was calm and still potent. But his nose didn't crinkle. He didn't mention anything or show any significance of disenchantment with us.

"Trust is something to be earned," he said. "I am in this room alone with you ladies because I trust you to understand I mean you no harm." He turned and shouted. "Open!"

Within seconds, the latch to our room was pulled back into the wall and the door slowly swung open.

"Mother has the bathing area ready for you. The men and I will escort you." He shared.

The heavy and deep sighs in the room had a few break out into applause. We all grew big smiles, excited to get ourselves clean. He won each of us over easily. I was going to have a bath or shower. I didn't care which one at this point. They could hose me down, for all I cared.

UNDER PRESSURE

The pressure of the warm water was enough to help massage the knots out of my back and shoulders. I stood naked with my lower back enjoying the stream of fresh warm water on my head and run down my body. My mid-length brown hair draped on each side of my neck. I rubbed my face, washing off what little makeup residue that lingered on my skin. I could feel the grit of dirt being washed away as my smooth skin emerged from the clean water.

The stone floor and walls were heated. This was meant to comfort us, enjoy the privilege of showering. There was built in soap dispensers and shampoo bars tucked inside the walls at each shower station. We were all out in the open, vulnerable in groups of ten.

The shampoo bar smelled of coconut as I gripped it and rubbed it on my hair and felt that lathering build up. My nails massaged and scrubbed my scalp and I couldn't remember something like this was euphoric to my body. I breathed in deeply reminiscing when Brant and I snuck in our showers together. Remembering his soft touch as his fingers glided over my body. How he gently washed me and in-between kisses the soap lathered on my back and neck.

His tall figure would block the stream and I would feel the draft, I would reach around and turn up the heat and he complained it scorched his body. Then he would allow me to stand in front of the stream of hot water as he massaged my scalp with the soap. It was a delicacy of mine as I melted into his body, my knees weakened, and I would turn around to wrap my arms around him and deeply kiss him.

My palm rested on the warm shower wall. The water running over the crown of my head and the warmth run down my body. Knowing I wouldn't know when I would be in Brant's arms like that again, my other hands gripped my skin over my heart.

The shower automatically turned off. We were warned we would only have time for a six-minute shower and I was able to get everything washed and rinsed and still had time to reminisce and long for my husband. Most women whined and mumbled under their breaths as we began to walk in the other side of the room as instructed and the next set of women would enter to take their shower.

As we exited, the floor was colder as we entered into the woman's powder room. Towels were set on the walls, a note stating we can only take one. We shivered as we transferred from the warm shower stalls, leaving the heated floors to walk through the thick drape and into the powder room with a cold marble floor.

Mother was there to hand us garments one by one as we entered. She handed them to us nicely folded and a ribbon tied around to keep them in place. With her cheery disposition, her voice chimed as she greet all of us and didn't waver that none of us returned the favor.

My eyes immediately went to the crystal chandelier with flickering LED candles. The shadow on the green vine ceiling looked like thin tree branches stretching across. The walls were a smooth texture that was designed to resemble a Roman outdoor bath.

Towels wrapped around our bodies and some decided to wrap their hair and walk naked. My hand touched the painted stone on the vines, traced along the wall, needing to make myself believe this was real, my reality. My hair dripping wet from the shower, I felt the trickle of the water run down my body and onto the floor. I shuffled my feet so I wouldn't slip and fall on the cold and went marble floor.

I counted ten vanity mirrors against the wall and on the other side were ten curtain stalls for us to enter and dress into. We were instructed to get dressed and then comb our hair and if we wished to throw our hair in a style, there were ribbons.

Feeling like cattle at this point. I was quiet. No words were exchanged among us. My solemn eyes noticed I wasn't the only one who felt as dreaded. The shower was pleasant and made me feel refreshed and clean, but now that was over, I feared what the next step was.

Stepping into my private dressing booth to get dressed, the curtain was pulled closed behind me as Mother quickly made her rounds. The stiff cotton plain clothes were in between my hands. Mother reminded us that we only had six minutes and the next group was to come in.

I set the clothes on the shelf, pulled the curtain behind me and stared at the clothes. My hair dripping wet onto the floor, the cold temperature of the marble floor now made me shiver. My hand went to reach and untie the ribbon to look at the garments, but by putting on these garments, would mean I would further accept whatever this was. I pulled my hand back, as my arms tightened around the towel.

My ears perked up at the other women on each side of me grunting and rustling with the clothes. I took a step back. They were just clothes, I shouldn't be afraid. But, they weren't my choosing. I would never wear whatever was given to me and a part of me didn't want to know what it looked like. I took another step back. I should run out of the room and refuse the clothes.

Naked? Are you an idiot? Put the damn clothes on and find a way to escape this place! My subconscious yelling at me. I questioned myself again. *Where would I go?*

Running naked around this place? What was I thinking. Not only would I draw more attention to myself, in this heavily guarded place, my luck, I would run right into Hunter. I'm sure he would enjoy chasing me around and having my naked body within his grasp. My body shivered at the thought.

I stepped forward, grabbed the ribbon and untied it to reveal my garments inside. There was a an adjustable bra and large what I considered granny panties I put on first. Not my style, but they were soft to the touch and would do the job. I was thankful we didn't have to wear corsets. Those were painful and always took two people to get into.

I wondered if Mother advocated for us when it came to the garments. *Being a woman herself, no man would have put that much detail into our clothing.*

My dress skirts came in a few layers that confused me at first. The first layer was a long black skirt to tie over my waist with another brown wrapping. Then my long cream colored sleeved shirt that was tight around the waist, but my sleeves were wide at my wrists.

"Does anyone get how to put these on?"

I heard the frustrated voice shout next to me. She had been grunting and moaning the entire time.

"I'll assist you. Two minutes ladies." Mother shouted as she pulled back the curtain next door to help.

I guessed as best as I could and when I stepped out, Mother was pleased with my look and helped adjust my top brown to overlay around my cream shirt to make it appear this was one seamless dress.

At the vanity station, Amara was already there as her long chestnut hair was braided and draped on one shoulder. She wanted me to come and sit so she could do my hair. Her overlay skirt was an orange, my eyes scanned to see other colors to help set us apart, everything else about our looks were nearly the same.

As Amara was eager and sweet enough to work on my hair. As I stared at myself into the mirror, it was the women behind me that I watched. It was evident his Grace hand-picked vulnerable, lonely women. Tracing back to last night and listening to their stories, they were all women who had no attachments to anyone. *Who would really miss them?*

Thinking about Reynard, the first face I saw coming into this place. Just before the injection, as I was cradled in his arms, he called me Rebecca. Why would he call me Rebecca? He might have had the wrong information, but I seemed to be the only one with a family, husband and children who would miss me.

I heard Ozzy's voice inside my head.

"You have children? A husband?"

Then, remembering the pause, the struggle as he had to think about doing the right thing, but he cursed under his breath.

"Sorry…Looks like we don't have a choice."

Clearly they were suppose to kidnap Rebecca and I must have looked like her. I hated Rebecca now. She was supposed to be here, not me! I wasn't sure when I should share this information. If it was safe to. What if this makes his Grace or

Mother embarrassed and I'm tossed in the locker to be forgotten.

"There!" Amara said. "Your hair looks beautiful."

Amara tightened the last bit as half my hair was pulled up, twisted and laid flat at the top of my crown. I thanked her and quickly escorted out of the room as the next set of ladies were about to enter.

THE HARD TRUTH

Patience is the word I need to remind myself daily as I live in this place. What I needed to do was watch my surroundings, remember the faces, stay quiet and listen to discussions around me. Earlier, if I would have raised hell and refused to wear the clothing, I would only ask for trouble.

Amara told me she hadn't seen her travel companion when she raised a stink, of what, I didn't recall, but still. It had been days and was she starved? Was the locker truly a scary place? Those weapons the Watchmen carried were made specific for this place. Getting tased didn't look fun and I didn't want to find out. What I needed to do was outsmart these people.

I was a logically and patient woman. It was a strong attribute of mine and a weakness. Because I was always careful and calculated, I didn't react like how others should. In fact, thinking about all the women in this place, no one was truly defiant or seem to cause trouble.

If these women were hand picked, then this must be a

quality his Grace took into account. Fearful women who were submissive. Yes, a few voiced their opinion, but there was no yelling, throwing items or fighting with the Watchmen. No one was kicking or screaming. This was a calculated move on his Grace's part. How would he have known this information?

A new Watchman I had not seen before stood outside of the room that led to another long hallway. He was tall, with a California sun kiss tan. His straight blonde hair at his shoulders glistened as the rays came through the windows. His long square jaw protruded with a dimple in his chin. His eyes were small and seemed to squint like he always had a pondering thought.

His enormous hand wrapped around the top of his weapon, ready to pull out and turn on at any second.

"They keep getting bigger." I leaned to Amara.

"Agreed. Plus, more good-looking." She smiled.

I nudged her in the shoulder trying not to smile.

"Ladies, this is Wallace. He will escort you, please follow." Mother said quickly, she rushed back in to help the other women coming from the showers.

Amara and I glanced at one another and mouth the name Wallace.

"Yum." Amara said.

Wallace turned swiftly and walked down the hall. The rest of us quickened our pace to keep up with him. His firm legs took long strides.

Wallace opened the dining room hall door. The muscles on his arm flexed an enormous bulge as he held the heavy door.

"Ladies." Wallace said. His eyes looking over our heads.

Meeting with the other women who came before us. Amara and I were welcomed as the twins waved in our direction and gestured they saved us a seat. The heavy door closed and locked at the echo of the latch as the metal scraped down on the other side.

Everyone smelled fresh and clean. The smiles everyone carried now made the energy in the room hospitable.

"What do you think of Wallace?" Yasmin bit her bottom lip.

"Delicious." Amara matched Yasmin's giddy mood.

Since we were the second to the last group from showering and getting ready, we didn't have to wait long. About twenty minutes later, Wallace opened the door and the last set of women came in dressed like the rest of us with fresh faces and smiles of feeling clean.

The teasing scent of the fresh food being cooked in the back of the kitchen wafted its way into the room. My stomach gurgled smelling the fresh bread and sweet meat seared in the back. My mouth salivated. I didn't care what was going to be served.

The dining hall door opened once more and Mother glided into the room quick on her heels and on the stage with a big, bright smile.

"Ladies of Silver Pine, it is time for you to begin the rest of your life."

Her arms outstretched to welcome us all. I believe she was waiting for a standing ovation and quickly recovered when none of us knew how to react.

"Because we're clean, we should praise her?" Amara said, leaning to me, and crossing her arms.

I thinned my lips, dipped my head down to avoid laughing. We straightened up as soon as I saw a new Watchmen make his presence known at the end of our table with a hard expression. His dark, charcoal complexion and beady white eyes made all of us button our mouthes to sit up straight.

His small rectangle face seemed squish together with his small forehead, eyes sunken in, big wide nose and plumped lips that stuck out from the rest of his face. Like all the others, his tall stature and muscular physique showed prominent muscles on his body that the others did not have. His neck was short, but the bulge over his shoulder blades and well defined veins along his arms in every way made him intimidating.

Mother stayed in character and made her way down the stage to walk down the aisles. The click of her heels resonated on the stone floor.

"You ladies have been through too much. We are here to make it better. I would like you all..."

She paused taking notice of a woman staring at her with a hard expression, and arms crossed. Mother calmly addressed the women with her hands clasped.

"You are not happy?"

"You are not my mother!" The disgruntled woman barked. "I will not stand for you or for whatever this is! I want to go home!"

The woman was closer to the stage from my view. I saw her skin flush a sunburnt red. Her tone made most of us react in worry as my heart raced in my chest.

Mother's lips thinned. "I am your mother. You will do as your mother says, or you will go into the locker. Is that what you want?"

"My heart is going to burst through my chest," Amara whispered to me. "I don't want all of us to be punished for her outburst."

Feet shuffled on the floor. I turn to see more Watchmen come into the room and stood guard against the tapestry walls. They slowly pulled their weapons from their belts. Preparing for anything that could happen.

In near perfect unison, the static sounds of electricity on their weapons were turned on. There was gasps, whimpers amongst us. The nerves in my body raced as my eyes darted around the room to see and keep guard of their reaction.

Mother remained calm. A few guards went to rush over, when Mother rose her hand suggesting to stop, and stand back. The young woman sat with her arms crossed.

Mother took a step toward the woman. The others around her scooted away, which left the disgruntled woman vulnerable in her stand against this place.

"Valeria, please don't make this harder than it has to be," Mother told her.

Valeria's body stiffened at the sound of her name. She sucked up a short breath with a hand to her lips. She shook her head.

"I have a family back home."

Mother shook her head as she knelt. "No you don't. Your mother drank herself to death a few years ago and left you with your brother, a previously convicted drug abuser. He sold you to a sex-traffic group where you were high on morphine and raped on a nightly basis."

Tears streamed down Valeria's face. It was clearly a painful reminder, especially to have someone else know her secret and share it out loud. We all watched how Mother's words had visibly weakened the woman's spirit.

Without missing a beat, Mother continued.

"You escaped and came to Florida. You picked yourself up and tried to get on your feet, but again you were taken advantage of, by a boyfriend who beat you and left you to die in a city park. You were homeless, down on your luck and had nowhere else to go."

Mother took Valeria's hand in hers. "We can be your home, your true family. There is no one here who will do the things you survived. Accept your new life and let go of the past."

Valeria's shoulders slumped, her head down. There was

no argument. Mother slowly got to her feet as she held onto Valeria's hand.

"You all were given abysmal lives out in that world. Here, you have a second chance. A new beginning without having the world judge you."

The sniffles around me grew. My eyes carefully glanced seeing the tear stained faces. Listening to everyone else relate, mentally break down was giving Mother the fuel she needed to get her point across.

"Yes, this is new…your past life is no longer yours to bare. Together, we can rebuild our new home, and make new families. You wont have to worry about dead-end jobs, paying bills, society dictating what to like and what not. There is no more feeling rejected by social media…"

Her lips curved at those who reached out to her. "I am not your enemy. Your Mother is not that kind of person. You will not have to want for anything. We are all equal in Silver Pines."

In the eyes of others, it was like seeing an angelic Angel for the first time touch down on Earth. Promising them safety and salvation. Hope in their big wide eyes as the tears fell off their faces. It was like she was giving them self-worth.

I even saw this as my head turned in Amara's direction. I leaned in to whisper.

"Don't give in."

Amara wanted to crack a smile. "I'm not as desperate." She winked back, but I could see the hesitation.

Mother turned a corner and began to walk down our aisle. The sunlight through the stained glass cascaded down as though the streaks from Heaven above blessed her with her words. There was a glow, an aura to her stride coming down to us.

My body straightened up as she came closer. Her plump lips stretched to reach out to the women and squeeze their hands back. When she looked at me, her smile faded. In the back of my mind, I was probably the only one who wasn't buying this charade.

It was a smart move on her part I noted to myself. Being down here with us, not on stage like a dictator would, and tell us what to do. She was the one who wanted to make sure we were on equal grounds, like she said to us. This was a classic move from a cult leader perspective.

Now, the whole room wanted to know what was next. The fear I felt before from everyone else's energy faded. Mother was full aware she had the attention in the room going in her favor.

"Ladies, you were selected to be here. You are the people that will help nourish our community. His Grace met thousands of people and saw the potential in you that others in your past refused to see."

Mother stopped and stood in front of Amara. Her thin fingertips grazed Amara's cheek, she spoke softly.

"You all wanted a second chance at life. We are offering you this chance."

Amara's eyes closed as a tear slid down her cheek. She looked up at Mother, like the rest of them.

"Thank you." Amara whispered to Mother as she grasped her hand and squeezed.

Mother continued her pace. The weight of my chest rested easier as she walked in the opposite direction.

"You will be assigned rooms," she announced. "Your new life with us begins today."

MY NAME IS

On our way out of the dining hall. There was new and fresh faces of women helping as a table sat in the middle of the hallway. They wore the same garments that we did and they passed out items we stood in line for as we were to receive our room assignments.

First, I was given a forest green wool blanket, with cream colored sheets. A goose feather pillow plopped on top as the line was moving. The three women helping were all smiles, warm and welcoming. Their long dark hair was pulled back halfway. They were angelic, like Mother.

The smell of fresh linen that sat in the sun to dry reminded me of my time at my grandmother's house. I could never forget this smell. It was a fresh breeze of pine in the air and green grass. I squeezed the items against my chest and inhaled deeply at the warm memory.

These were the only articles I could now call my own. My bare feet ached on the cold stone floor, as Amara and I side stepped toward the last table where Mother came around to assign us to our living arrangements.

Reynard approached from the other end of the hallway to

stand behind Mother. He was like a wax doll standing still, look over our heads and not at anyone.

Amara turned around and smiled at me. I sensed she was taking a liking to Reynard, because when he was close, her face brightened and so did her mood.

We could pick up small lavender pouches at the end of one table. This scent reminded me of my sister's back home. Everything about her was lavender. She was obsessed with it. She taught me many years ago to put a bag in my pillow and it would help me sleep.

Feeling the bag, inhaling the fresh, dried scent. If this made me sleep easier at night, and would make me think of her strength. This is what I needed. The line was moving at a slow pace. At the end of the hall, groups were forming so we could be escorted to our rooms.

I began to daydream that I was walking out the front door to my Southern California home. I was being dragged by Reynard and Hunter. When I was able to glance back, I saw Brant and the boys standing at the door with confused faces. They didn't move from the home. Brant didn't race out to come rescue me, he stood confused, watching me leave.

I snapped back into my new reality and sucked in a sharp breath. The adrenaline of anticipation made me twitch. The unknowing of my fate made my mouth dry. Everything around me was moving in slow motion.

Mother gave me a smile as I approached the table. She stared at me for a few seconds longer. I thought she asked me a question I didn't hear because I was day dreaming. Then, something in her memory clicked and she searched through her index cards in her neatly carved wooden box of information. She handed me my parchment.

"Thank you Rebecca. I see your—"

"My name is not Rebecca." I interrupted.

Without a second thought I blurted out my name. I

decided right then and there, I would be damned to try and portray to be someone else. In this moment, I didn't care what happened. I felt like a fool, but with so many witnesses, they couldn't get mad at me.

With everything his Grace and Mother shared about not being afraid, accept this fate, how we were all chosen. All the women knew I was Liz. After being stripped and taken to some desolate place, I would be Liz, not Rebecca. My hand tried to hand her parchment back.

Mother seemed to be studying my face. She asked Reynard for his tablet. She scanned through and typed with her finger tips. When she held the tablet up to compare the image of Rebecca and myself, she saw something.

After a few more seconds, Mother answered me. "No... no, you're not. Your name?"

"Elizabeth Ann Thomas." I stiffened my shoulders with pride, to say my name out loud was a relief because I wasn't who they thought I was. "My married name is Thomas."

Mother set down the tablet and I saw a picture of another woman, she had my face but there were slight difference. Her eyes were hazel, mine are green and her face looked a bit longer in the jaw line with a pointed chin.

Mother's finger tips touched the tablet. She continued to study me. "Elizabeth—"

"I'm Liz for short." I don't know why I felt the need to snap at her. She wouldn't have known that fact about me.

Mother stood slowly to her feet.

"Liz," she said, correcting herself. "I think you and I need to get something straightened out."

THE HALLWAYS WERE quiet and looked like every other arched hall, with paintings of His Grace and or what I could assume what our community would appear to look like outside these walls. Alcoves were cut out as giant LED candles were made to have some sort of light instead of the burning smell of wick. Even in the daylight, there wasn't a lot of light in the halls. Every corner or around an alcove had darkness with shadows stretching out into the light as it was appearing to grab a hold of other shadows.

Pine needle wreaths were displayed on flat edges near the window for a refreshing scent. It helped kick up my senses when inhaled into my lungs. The scent was just as invigorating inside the body, like breathing fresh air.

My feet scurried behind Mother who held up her dress skirts trying to match the pace of Reynard. With all the twist and turns, I couldn't have found way back if I tried.

The last corner, was different because there was warmth from the large cove windows with the sun cascading through. I was asked to take a seat at the single stool that sat on the outside of the room and told to wait.

I did what was asked as Mother and Reynard entered the room and quickly closed the door behind them. I couldn't see anything else useful. For the first few minutes I sat with my back straight and hands on my lap. After more time had gone by, my back slowly laid against the wall for support. My nail beds began to glide together. The sound was like rubbing a string of pearls together. I did this whenever I was alone, nervous or anxious.

The wooden stool was cushioned and fairly new. I bounced waiting to hear a creak, but it was firm. My ears perked up at the commotion from outside the walls. I heard men heave and shout in unison, they counted from one to three. My curiosity led me to the stained glass window of a giant tree with deep roots. My finger tips touched the glass to take a closer look as I saw men gathered around lifting something heavy. The color glass blurred images, it hurt my eyes to focus on. I heard grunting as they pulled at something together. Wood creaked as something flat was being pulled up.

There faces were distorted in the glass. The difference was hair color, possibly, height and weight. Even through glass like this, I didn't trust my eyes.

"Elizabeth." Reynard's deep voice startled me. His annoyed expression me near the window quickened his pace as he came over, gently grab me by the arm and pull me away.

"Don't ask for trouble," he quietly reminded me. "You will need to go in and plead your case to his Grace."

Reynard brought me as my eyes were pleased to see the architecture and artifacts of this ornate room. From floor to ceiling there were books and shelves of decorated antique artifacts from the medieval era. Scrolls, iron helmets, and weapons. My eyes scanned the room quickly, needing to soak up my surroundings.

His Grace stood by the fire place. The smell of wood burning with charcoal overpowered the pine scent from the hallway. The fireplace was nearly as tall as Reynard with the red and burnt giant logs of wood. The limestone and dark granite arched solid wall of art. A giant portrait of his Grace mimicked the last famous picture of King Henry the VIII.

His Grace had his back to me. I couldn't tell what kind of mood he would be in. Mother stood near the crystal window. Surrounding the window was green glass of artwork of vines, but I could clearly see the beautiful blue sky and the fluffiest clouds.

Mother turned to me and held out both arms. She sauntered over and gave me a hug.

"My darling lady. We are sorry for this unfortunate situation."

She squeezed and brought me to sit on the couch in the

middle of the room. The red velvet couch was stiff as a board.

Mother sat next to me and held her hands in mine.

"Elizabeth. We will need you to be honest and tell us your story."

Her big eyes were comforting filled with sorrow and wonder. I chose to be careful with my words.

"Where do you want me to begin?" I didn't want to fall into a trap.

MISTAKE

"Where were you taken?" His Grace turned around to face us.

"I was in Seattle with my husband." My lips quivered at the painful memory.

His Grace wore a heavy embroidered royal attire with his puffed out purple sleeves. An emerald green long tunic lined with animal fur. His waist belt was aligned with emerald jewels. It truly was an exquisite attire, that looked very costly. This portrayal of elaborate customer and tailored outfits was to show who he was and what we were. I was a peasant compared to him, Mother and even the Watchmen.

It was disgusting and disgraceful. This man played with real human lives. His arrogance believing he could kidnap victims, and make everyone believe in a different way of life sickened me. I cleared my throat, holding in my anger. Accusing him, yelling at him, would only have me thrown into the locker and it could be until my last breath.

Play this smart, Liz.

My eyes gazed down to my hands. Mother's hands were on top of mine and she gave a slight squeeze. When my eyes drifted up to meet hers, she shifted her eyes towards his Grace.

"We were touring the Chihuly Gardens, after the tour I needed to use the restroom. The one in the building had a long line, I was directed by an employee to go outside the gardens to another set."

"You were visiting, you didn't work there?" His Grace asked. I shook my head. "You were with your husband?" He proceeded.

I nodded. "Yes."

Before his Grace could ask, Reynard supplied him with a tablet. He eager fingers pressing, scrolling, his eyes reading and then he seemed to compare. The color of his face changed with his eyes shifting back to me and then the tablet. He held up the tablet next to my face.

"Remarkable." His Grace handed the tablet back to Reynard. "Classic case of mistaken identity. The eyes are the wrong color and the face shape is slightly different." He scuffed. "You have a small beauty mark near your lips as the Rebecca we needed, did not. Your nose is slightly thinner..."

As he continued to name the difference between Rebecca and I, listening to him compare her to me shortened my temper.

"Are you going to free me?" I snapped.

I removed my hands away from Mother. I was tired of their games since I was clearly not supposed to be here. I jumped to my feet.

Reynard was prepared and ready to use his weapon on me. His Grace put a hand to stop him. Mother stiffened to my sudden stance.

The green is his Grace's eyes were dull with his age. I figured he was close to being forty. The soft crow-lines from his eyes where a hairline lighter than his sun-kissed skin. His neatly trimmed beard showed a few gray hairs and his lips were thin. Standing this close to him, I was able to see more into his square face as his matching jaws was the prominent feature to stand out.

He held up both hands in defense to me. I was worked up, my shoulders breathing as the pace of my pounding heart. My hands clenched at my sides.

"Did the woman you travel with know your story?" His Graced asked.

"I didn't travel with a woman. I was with a man."

My breathing shallowed a bit. I was honest and was not sure if this would work in my favor. His Grace shot a sharp glance to Reynard who swallowed a big lump in his throat.

"I will see if this is true, your Grace," Reynard quickly responded.

We both knew he was aware since my arrival. My lips parted to mention how he knew from the incident of mine and Zak's arrival, and how Zak put up a fight and I tried to run and escape. But, telling on Reynard would not win me any favors if this wasn't going to go in the direction I am hoping for.

"Why would I lie?" This clearly got me frustrated. "I am not supposed to be here, that is apparent."

My heart thumped harder in my chest, my cheeks flushed and my eyes wanted to water. My hands clenched so tight, I could feel the edges of my nails dig into the palms of my skin.

"This is an unfortunate burden that has been placed upon you." His Grace's voice tried to be kind and comforting. "I'm sorry for the misfortune you being taken away from your husband—"

"And children." I added.

Blinded by the news, his Grace stepped back. "Children?"

He snapped his look over to Mother who was already on

the tablet pressing hard on the screen and swiping through notes.

This could be my way out? Recalling the stories I picked up on the last night of other women didn't seem to be married or have children. If a man like his Grace went to great lengths to preconceive a masterful plan where the woman were to be child barring, I might be considered damage goods, and be let out of this mess.

For the first time in my life. I didn't see my condition as a weakness, but this could mean this was my saving grace. It was a terrible way to think of myself, but if it meant my freedom. I could suck up my pride.

Mother set the tablet down. "I don't even know why I am looking. These results are from Rebecca. We will need to obtain Liz's medical history."

It was the sudden sparkle in his eye, an idea popped into him.

"You've born children?" His Grace asked.

I felt stuck. If I lied, they would examine me. If I told the truth about my condition, they could release me because I would be no use to whatever he had planned.

"I have not." I answered swallowing the lump in my throat. "I am unable to have children. I am a step-mother to my boys."

His Grace seemed to ponder my situation as he turned and walked toward the fireplace. His fore-finger and thumb rubbed the hair on his chin.

"Why are you unable to have children?" His voice was curious.

"I suffer from a biocornuate uterus." No matter how many times I repeated it, my illness I bore, stung.

His Grace met my gaze and dropped. Then he glanced over to Mother for a second before looking back and meeting my eyes.

"My uterus is a heart shape, which means I can get pregnant but—"

"You cannot carry to term," Mother said, finishing my sentence.

She placed a hand over her stomach. The dismal words saddened her, like a broken record.

His Grace rushed over at Mother's knees. He gently held her hands in his.

"We prayed for a sign. What if this is it?" The whispered words he said to her made blood drain from my head. His head snapped in my direction. "Have you been consulted for surgery?"

Oh God! No! I wanted to scream. I could feel the sweat run down my back. My chest tightened. I didn't want them tearing into my body and be some experiment. My feet stepped back. My eyes glanced around the room for a sudden thought of how I could escape. The window behind me was fitting, only problem, I probably wasn't strong enough to break through, I'm sure Reynard would be quicker and grab me before I got close.

"We will need to consult with the doctor." Mother said speaking to his Grace.

My ears didn't want to hear anything more. My back bumped into something soft and yet solid. Reynard stood behind me and shook his head. I didn't even pay attention to his movements and he seemed to be aware of what I was trying to do.

His Grace got to his feet and walked in my direction. "I wish our meeting was under better circumstances. Fate has brought you to me."

My nose was consumed by his smell of wood, lemon, mint, and pepper grapefruit.

"Reynard, make sure Liz is taken care of," his Grace brushed by me and left all of us in the room.

My knees weakened, I dropped and wept into my hands the second the door closed behind his Grace. I lost all my emotions as the tears and anguish poured out from my broken heart.

I heard heels come closer and Mother was the last person I needed.

"Leave me alone!" I screamed holding my heart. "Don't you understand? I'm not supposed to be here!" The depths of my lungs exhausted every ounce of air.

I felt the veins in my neck pulse and my skin heated from the anger.

Reynard's big leather boots stood near me. His authoritative voice said something, but I was crying so loud, my lungs were out of sync from my body. I choked on the air my body was trying to breathe in. The door opened and closed quickly.

Reynard's knees cracked as he bent down to speak to me. "I am sorry for this mistake, but you must find a way to move forward with your new life."

He allowed me to cry it out. With one leg bent as the other on the ground, he stayed there until my body and mind were exhausted from knowing my fate.

This whole time I was an idiot to perceive this would work in my favor. This what happens when one does not react! I was pissed at myself because my sister wouldn't have tolerated this. She would have fought off the guys from the very beginning and wouldn't have been thrown in the van.

If she was in the train with Zak, she would have pushed him to find an escape route. I relied on others and trusted in them and I was in this position, because I didn't fight hard enough.

From this moment, I made myself a promise. As I pushed myself off the floor, Reynard wanted to help me to my feet, but I shrugged his gesture away.

There was no use in crying on the floor and having a pity party. I took the bottom of my apron and wiped my tears and stood on my feet. I would no longer be weak. They don't know it yet, but I would find my own way out of this place. I would return home to my husband and children.

ROOMMATES

Mentally, I was numb. I was now in what they called survivors mode. I was thinking back to some articles I read on survivors of kidnapped victims. How they dealt with the trauma. It was allowing your capture to let them think they have all the power.

As my feet followed Reynard back to the women's tower, when he spoke to me, I didn't reply. I wasn't even listening to him. After a few more attempts, he gave up and we remained in silent until he brought me to Mother.

On the grounds, the journey to the tower seemed to stretch farther and farther away. The air was warm as the sun was setting. I wasn't taken into account of where I was going, or what anything else in my surroundings looked like. I stared blankly and went through the forward motion.

In the article I remembered tearing up reading how some survivors needed to tuck a portion of their soul away to endure whatever came their way. Everyday was about planning it out slowly, getting the kidnapers to eventually trust them.

Don't try to outsmart them right away!

It was about trying to get through each day. How to keep yourself in a mode where there was always hope. Trust in your instincts and don't jump at easy attempts, be smart.

MOTHER WAITED for Reynard and myself outside the women's tower. She held up her hand to him as he approached.

"I will take it from here." She said.

Reynard bowed his head and continued on. Mother carefully approached me. Her eyes scanning my face, matching my sorrow with hers.

"I'm sorry." Her words just above a whisper.

My eyes were puffy and sore. We would be loosing light and last thing I wanted was to have a chat with this woman. When I didn't respond, she nodded, picked up her skirts and asked me to follow along.

I was completely and eternally numb. My feet carried me, but I didn't pay attention to anything. Mother led the way and said something back to me from time to time. She knew I wasn't paying attention, there was no feeling left in me. I was just an existing body following her around.

"This way."

She picked up her skirts as we approached a set of spiral stairs. Small almond shaped windows every sixth step led up to the next floor and I could see the thin glass in between, viewing the outside world. The glow of the sunset behind the mountains was now a beautiful creamsicle orange in the West.

On the second floor there was a vast opening in the center to show all around each sides and corridors along the wall. Wood railings were a sturdy oak. I looked up to see two more stories in this section of the castle was directly above me with the same wood railings.

My mind was beginning to think in dark thoughts. *I could accidentally fall from the fourth floor.* If I couldn't find a way out to escape, I might have to succumb to my emotional state of mind.

"Let me show you to your room."

Mother fumbled with big iron keys. *Every detail...* taking notice at the what looked to be sixteenth century keys made for our locked doors. I heard laughter and women talking as we passed by the long loft of rooms.

Stopping at the left corner at the end, Mother stuck the key in the door and gave a slight tap.

"This is your living quarters for the time being."

The iron key unlocked with a loud *clunk.* Mother pushed the door open and the women's voices inside shushed as we entered.

"Liz!" Amara was excited to see me and rushed over for a hug.

The strong scent of gardenia's was a warm welcome. When she pulled back from me, she knew something was terribly wrong.

Yasmin and Esther weren't blind and noticed my tear stained face, blotchy skin and puffy eyes. They gave me a small wave in unison. Their eyes saddened with worry.

Mother cleared her throat. "I thought these ladies were a good fit to lift your spirits. I shall leave you alone. Tomorrow is another day."

When the door closed, I heard the *clunk* of the lock that sealed me into this room. I felt a daydream of seeing the door close to my own house as I was being hauled away from my last imaginary dream. Before the door to my house closed, Brant and the boys were sad. The sound of the lock closing was metaphorical to the door to my life almost closing on itself.

Taking a look at my new surroundings, the space for all four of us couldn't have been bigger than a normal size child's bedroom. Two sets of handcrafted oak bunk beds, one on each side of the room. Two matching sets of dressers side by side and four walls.

I didn't know what depressed me more, continuing on with the charade that this is my life, or my new sleeping arrangements.

Amara carefully approached me. Her hand at the bottom of my back, she led me over to point out she made my bed.

"Also…" she grabbed a nightgown that sat on my pillow. "I hope that was alright?"

I stood still, staring at the bed. I know I was making an uncomfortable silence.

"You can have the top or bottom bunk, doesn't matter to me." Amara offered.

She was trying to get me to say something. My eyes felt the pressure as they stretched and moved in her direction. I made my way over pressed my hand down on the soft goose feather woven mattress.

"No metal springs." One of the twins said behind me.

"We have assigned drawers, and clothes in our size." Amara pulled open the top drawer on the far left side. "Since I got the top bunk, I thought you should have the top drawer." She faintly smiled.

My head peaked over to see socks, underwear and dress garments. As my thin fingers reached out to touch the clothes. Amara gently settled me onto my bed.

"What happened?" She asked.

Yasmin and Esther sat across from me on the bottom bunk, eager to know. Amara sat next to me, one hand wrapped around my shoulder.

"I'm a classic case of mistaken identity. They said I must except my new life here."

My tone was solemn, just like how Mother's was not long ago.

"Did his Grace say why we are all here?" Amara asked.

I shook my head. "No more than what we've already been told. He didn't like the fact I was a married woman and I have two sons."

"Have you noticed that no one else seems to be married?" Esther said to the group.

"So, then it's true. This is a cult," Amara crossed her arms. "This is morbid though. We live in the past, but have the technology to be in the present? Why?"

"My guess, to start a new civilization." Yasmin pointed out.

That made the rest of us visibly uncomfortable. But it gave the four of us a spark of discussion.

"If we were all kidnapped, then there is going to be a heavy amount of disappearing cases." Amara said.

Yasmin shook her head. "I disagree."

"Because?" Amara asked.

"No one knows in our family what happened to us, because we ran away years ago." Esther said.

"From the sound of it, seems like the women in this place is in a situation like us. No family, no real friends, no social media." Yasmin pointed out.

"No one is going to miss me either." Amara realized. "So, we are the misfits of society."

"I was taken in Seattle and so was Zak." I pointed out.

"I was in the Bahamas on a vacation I won." Amara said.

"We were in New York." Yasmin and Esther said in unison.

The odds were even more against us at this point. My eyes closed, knowing the hard truth.

"Over twenty-one hundred people are reported missing everyday. That we know of, sixty of us were taken from different times and dates." I pointed out.

"Well just turn into another cold case." Amara said.

DAY ONE

The loud sound of a rooster crowing from a speaker in one corner of our bedroom made me bolt upright. I smacked my forehead on the upper bunk above me. My brain was already a mess emotionally, and now physically I was going to wear a knot on my forehead for a good portion of the day.

Yasmin and Esther tried not to laugh as they welcomed me a good morning.

"Good morning ladies. Please dress and meet me outside your rooms in thirty minutes." Mother's voice came from the speaker.

"Here's to day one."

Amara jumped from her bunk and landed on the floor. She saw the bump on my forehead and bit down on her lip.

"Yeah, I know." I tossed the covers off, stripped down and began dressing into our dresses from yesterday. I grabbed my clothes from yesterday, while I was talking with his Grace. Mother gave a lesson how we only have two outfits a week, so our clothes were meant to last.

I slipped my skirt on and my long sleeved shirt was next

as I wrapped it around my waist with the belt. I wasn't as perky like the twins were, but I mentally was working on trying to get myself in the right headspace to deal with waking up each morning.

WHEN WE WERE all dressed with time to spare, Yasmin was braiding Esther's hair. Amara paced the room, annoyed we couldn't leave when we wanted.

Sitting on my made bed, I bite down on my thumb nail. In my mind I was thinking of how I could get a plan in motion. What supplies would I need and should I give myself a timeline?

A soft and smooth beep came from the speaker and our doors automatically unlocked and drifted open. Yasmin jumped up and hurried over to open our door and peak outside to make sure it was alright.

Esther was tying off the end of her hair. "What are you afraid of now? You had to be the first one to open the door."

Yasmin waved off her sister. "At least I'm not the only one."

Across the hall, she waved at other women.

"Good morning ladies."

Mother's voice was heard from the first floor standing in the middle of the open space. She seemed pleased to see all of us women from all four stories look out from our open corridors and she was the center of attention.

"I see you are all dressed. You will be greeted each morning by our rooster. This will signify you have thirty minutes to dress and be down stairs to eat in the dining hall. Fourth floor, you may lead and come down first and then so on. We all must be in a line with our hands folded or clasped in front of us when walking."

Mother also seemed pleased to see how all of us were following her rules.

"Here we go." Amara said behind me.

Waiting for our floor to be told when to leave, I didn't notice Mother was standing in an open seating area and the shelves were filled what looked like the same navy blue binding of books. The tapestry hanging on the walls were a cream and faint blue floral patterns. Different shapes and sizes all connected in a beautiful vine display.

The art pieces hanging on the walls were of picturesque mountains in the background, valleys below and rivers flowing. A giant fire place was behind Mother, not yet lit. This must have been our own reading and gathering area for us.

Amara nudge me as I was a few paces behind. I quickened my pace and we made it down the stairs to the bottom floor, through the reading room and followed in the line to outside in the warm sunlight.

When my feet touched the cold stone to the bare grass outside leading to the dining hall, I sucked up a deep breath. The fresh air filled my lungs of gardenias. My eyes closed as the sun kissed my face. The sweet and tender sighs from others around me take in the sun and the scent of the outside world was a good start to the morning.

Halfway across the giant lawn centered in between, the smell of something sweet and sugary pleased my senses, making my toes curl and stomach growl.

MY WOODEN SPOON picked up a small portion of the honey oats with brown sugar. My lips eagerly ate the oatmeal as I added fresh blueberries and strawberries that sat in a bowl in the middle of our table. Mother slowly strolled up and down the aisles. Reminding us to sit up straight and to tilt our spoons to our mouths, allowing the oats and fruit to flow into our mouth. We were not to slurp with our lips.

"When finished, walk up to the small window. Whatever is left, you scrape out into the bin and set your bowls, cups and spoons inside on the belt."

As instructed, we got up intermittently to do so, Watchmen stood guard at the doors. Besides us, I wondered who else would be a threat they would need to protect us against.

When I approached the window. I had done the job and could have licked my bowl clean if needed. Reynard was at the entrance and I could feel his eyes on me. Glancing in his direction, he tilted his head to the right. I assumed he needed to see me on the other side, or outside?

Amara snuck up and tucked her arm with mine. "He truly is a nice specimen." She couldn't help but blush.

"Don't get in trouble." I warned.

Reynard was already walking to the right side of the room and he left through another regular door. I wanted to make sure I didn't miss my opportunity.

"I have to use the restroom."

I didn't give Amara a chance to reiterate. I made my way across the room and through the small regular door Reynard went through. I nearly crashed into him, he stood so close.

"Whoah! Geez! A little warning next time." I said.

Reynard stood with his arms folded over his chest. "I'm sorry."

"For what?"

"Your situation."

Caught off guard. I wasn't sure what to say.

"I thought you should know." He paused before he opened the door. He stared at the oval carved door. "I can't give you details, but, Zak wanted me to let you know he's ok."

My heart stopped. Reynard pushed the door open and as

my heart kickstarted in my chest, I was relieved to know Zak was alive.

After a few more seconds digesting the information. My hand pushed the door open. On stage, Mother waited patiently for all of us to take our seat to have our full undivided attention. When everyone in the room grasp the concept she was waiting on us, all eyes turned in her direction.

I tucked my hair behind my ear and quickly sat right next to Amara. I couldn't believe Zak was ok. I had been so worried. There was no way to pick out who he was, because I never laid eyes on him.

"You ok?" Amara leaned over.

I nodded. "Reynard just told me something."

Amara's eyes widened. After a moment of people sitting down and listening to Mother, she was eager to know.

"Go on."

"He said Zak wanted him to tell me, he was ok." I whispered.

Amara's mouth hung open.

"I'm happy to have you all in better spirits this morning," Mother said. "Each day will have its challenges and will also have blessings. Today is day one. You are going to be introduced to the other Faithfuls. Explore the greenhouse, see the lay of the land."

This made me think of how I could memorize or somehow draw out a map of this place.

The cheerful demeanor with her advantageous smile lifted most of the women's spirit in the room. They clapped, bright eyed and beaming with smiles.

"Follow me, my faithful followers." She waved as she made her way off the stage.

"Oh good, a field trip." I joked.

Amara held her mouth with her hand almost losing her

water. We allowed others to walk in front and remained toward the back. This gave me a better view of being able to see more and not worry about someone trying to educate me.

At the door, Hunter stood guard. When he saw me, he grinned. He tapped on the Wallace's shoulder as Amara and I were passing by. I heard his idea.

"Wallace. Reynard needs you more in the middle. I've got this back here." Hunter's deceiving voice said behind us.

Amara and I glanced at one another with worried expressions. We stayed close. Clearly my plans for scouting out the ground would have to wait, since now I could feel his eyes burning in the back of my skull. I kept my eyes forward. I wouldn't give him the satisfaction or attention.

Across the courtyard, on the other side of the state rooms, a giant green house was perfectly situation in a long rectangular glass with a peaked roof with solar panels mounting in the surrounding area.

Mother wore a microphone on her body, so no matter if I was in the front or back of the line. I heard her clearly.

Inside the greenhouse, the immediate feel was thick humidity. This easily had to have been the size of a football field. I was taken aback of all the sweet juicy fruits, orange and lemon trees. Strawberries and blue berries. On the other side was vegetables. Everything was labeled.

The sweet smell of dirt and food wafted in the air and all of us couldn't inhale enough as Mother walked through. We were educated to know about the beautiful solid wooden frame held up by the double panned side walls. The temperature controlled areas made it easy to stabilize the environment and misters up in rafters kept the area warm.

Amara pointed out to the medicinal area sectioned off.

"Look at that beauty." Her eyes lit up at the sight.

Both of us broke away from the group to check out the insulated and closed off area.

"You an herbalists?" I joked.

"Partial." She shrugged. "As a nurse, I studied—"

"Wait…" I interrupted. "You were a nurse outside these walls?"

She nodded with her big light brown eyes.

Glancing back, Hunter was occupied picking off an orange for himself to eat. I looked around and the group was walking toward the middle of the greenhouse, further away than where I wanted to be.

"We need to catch up." I said.

I felt someone close behind me as a hot breath was breathing down my neck and something poking my back.

"Do you know how badly I want to turn this on and give you a little zap," Hunter whispered in my ear.

My body stiffened. Amara's fearful expression locked with my matching eyes and we stayed still.

"We're not doing anything wrong." I whispered back with a tinge of annoyance.

He gripped my right shoulder and made me lean back into his chest. I felt his weapon press hard into my shoulder blades as his lips were centimeters from my neck. I could hear his nose sniff my skin and the back of my hair.

Amara went to say something. Hunter held my chin up. "Go on Amara, I want a reason for her to scream."

I winced in pain as he dug his weapon into the muscles of my shoulder blades. My eyes looked down to Amara. She was terrified to say or do anything. I shook my head.

"Seems a shower did you good." His grip loosened from my neck.

"Just do it!" I fired back, keeping my tone level.

"Why would you say that?"

The touch of his nose traveling from my shoulder and up

my neck hit me with a wave of disgust. I yanked away from his grip.

Surprised, Hunter seemed to like the feistiness I had in me.

"Where has this trait been?" The sly smile grew on his face.

He was quick to react and place his weapon on my stomach. My organs shook internally with disgust.

"Could be worth it. Both of us satisfying that electric force between us." Then he switched and quickly pointed it at Amara. "She looks like a good friend to watch us."

"Hunter?"

Mother's voice was heard closer to us than any speaker in the rafter could reverberate back to my ears.

"What is going on?"

She did not look pleased to see him so close to me.

"These two were talking and wandering around while you were giving the tour." He lowered his weapon. "They tried to argue with me."

Mother looked to Amara and myself for reassurance. Both of us lowered our heads, saying nothing. The last thing we wanted was to tell on him, he would have it out for us and make our lives even more miserable.

"Hunter, I need toward the front." Mother pointed and followed behind him as he made his way toward the front.

"He's going to be trouble for you," Amara whispered.

Our pace quickened to meet up with the others. "Don't I know it."

THE GROUNDS

My hand became my visor as I tried to see beyond the forest and lands when Amara and I stepped out from the greenhouse. It was a beautiful day with scattered white fluffy clouds. In the back of the greenhouse was land as far as the eye can see. No moat, no walls, but forest at every turn.

As the view was breathtakingly beautiful, I was keeping my eye out on Hunter. He stayed his distance from me, as Mother kept her eye on him. The long walk and tour of the green house was a lot of information to obtain. I never had a green thumb myself, but this was another serious investment his Grace spared no expense.

Mother picked up her skirts and was helped up on a rock with a flat piece so she could tower over everyone and speak to the group.

"Faithfuls like myself have been here for over half a year." Mother stated. "We came in phases to make sure what did and did not work. You will learn to live with one another, be taught the Faithful way, and make our village a thriving one."

The excitement and joy in her voice look to only enthuse

half the crowd. Amara and I in the back, were a part of the group that still remained skeptical.

I would have to play this smart. On the higher ground of the greenhouse and seeing vast forest that stretched for hundreds of miles. Thinking about running without a plan would be foolish. With the amount of cameras in this place, I'm sure every border was covered and could detect intruders. At least with my crime shows, it what I would have done.

Mother picked up her skirts to have us continue to walk around the greenhouse to see more of the village. The small inclines of dirt, stone paths and log cabins got me turned and twisted. This was not going to be easy, but I needed to outsmart not only Mother and his Grace, but trusted insiders.

The stone paths were impeded in the ground like they have been there for over a hundred years. Around the corner of the green house, was a small set of cabins. This was when we all saw for the first time the other men and women that were here before us, work their chores, go on about their day, talking amongst others like their normal daily lives.

It was like a field trip I had taken the kids once to an old ghost town and the actors pretended to reenact their staged settings. As we got closer, the incline of our walk was getting steep. To my surprise, the soft dirt didn't bother our feet. What was tiring was the thin air being inhaled in our lungs. This is the most all of us have walked in many days.

Breathing was getting harder and I felt the cramp on my right side. We stopped at the black smith as he gave us a wave and continued to bang on the metal he just pulled from the fire pit. There was a store front of the business and behind was his house with his wife.

The newly and smooth glossed over log cabin wore a giant horse shoe mounted on the outside of the entrance.

The smokey giant fire pit was in the middle of the entrance before the store front.

"Alex, would you like to introduce yourself to our last batch." Mother asked.

Trying to bring a smile to his face, Alex put down his tools. Grabbed a rag hanging from his belt and wiped his dirty, sweaty face. His appearance was truly deceiving, as he got closer, his height continued to grow. He was very tall, broad build with a small waist.

His loose cotton shirt had a deep v-neck as his brown chest hair protruded. The loose sleeves were rolled up to his elbows. His tied back dirty blonde hair made the features on his face striking. His beard was a touch darker than the hair on his head and he truly looked to me like a man from the mountains.

Alex gave a wave to us. "I'm Alex, my wife Elen and I have been a Faithful and were part of the first group. Life here can be hard at times because of the manual labor, but there is peace here."

His voice was deep, but clear. I even caught myself being drawn into his words. "We are family, we want for nothing. His Grace has changed our lives because outside these walls, it wasn't living, it was just existing to their standards. That wasn't me and certainly not my wife.

"Thank you Alex." Mother was pleased.

Alex waved us goodbye and continued to get back to his work. The sewing cabin was about thirty feet away nestled back from the black smith cabin. It had more pine trees surrounding it. A few steps up, Mother stood in the middle of the porch and turned to the crowd.

"Anyone familiar with sewing?"

Shyly, many hands rose around me. I felt a bit sided because I had done a terrible job as a child when my grandmother tried to teach me.

"We have a few designers who are with us and have made everything you see here." Mother bragged. "From our tapestries, to the clothes we wear on our backs. You will be asked from time to time to help."

A giant ball of yard was carved into the log cabin on the front. The same look as the black smith cabin, but less smoke stains. A corridor in the back of the house connected the two to another giant log cabin twice the size and two stories in height.

"The washing house is where we make our clothes, die them if needed, cut and wash our laundry." Mother pointed out. "This is also where our cleaning products come from made from all natural ingredients."

On our continued walk as we passed by, Mother was passionate about natural resources and how important it was for us to give back to the Earth.

A group of women carrying baskets of some type of cream colored sheets cut through the group. A blonde woman a bit more rounded in the face and hips took one look at me sideways and continued on. There was no smile or warmth to her.

"Did you do something to her outside these walls in your past life?" Amara snickered.

Feeling good I wasn't the only one who noticed the look with the group of women, we stayed close.

"I must have." My sarcasm quickly escaped my lips.

Continuing to walk up a small mound and away from the other cabins, a tall stone windmill sat on top as the blades were slowly turning with the breeze going by. A cabin with a peaked roof nestled close by.

"Our windmill is also our Weather service and technology station." Mother pointed out. "We have two onsite, and the other is below the castle grounds down the slope."

I stared at the three story smooth stone windmill. This

building was exactly the type of place that would have a lot of answers. I made a mental note to look for the person in charge of this windmill.

The turbines looked misplaced attached to the stone building. The long and thin blades were state of the art. They turned slowly, but the white blades had a solar glow to them and probably picked up signals from hundreds, if not thousands of miles away of incoming weather.

I nearly missed the group, when Amara tugged on my sleeve to continue. Leaving the place to head down the slope on the other side, Hunter's eyes were fixed on me. He shook his head as though he could read my mind. I tucked my hair behind my ears and quickened my pace to stay with the group.

Down a bit of the slope where the last building was, round and thick logs with a giant Red Cross carved on the front. It was the medical house for treatment, ailments and where medicine was going to be made.

I gasped to see the forty acres of farmland was at the bottom of the slope. The smooth texture of the dirt and giant barn house of many animals were segregated and caged in different areas looking down into it. Farm hands were laying out the hay by hand as a wagon with bails of hay walked along the edges so the cows could eat in their area.

The roof of the barn I noticed was painted a darker brown. The stall posts were a natural wood and the smooth boards were a burnt red, instead of the iconic color of bright red.

Mother wanted us to safely walk down the steep slope and use the carved out steps with thick pieces of timber to use as a guide and broke up the stairs going down.

Over looking farm land bewildered my imagination. Beyond the farm were houses tucked into the other side of a forest of small chimneys from the roofs billowed smoke stacks. This place was beyond any type of cult living I had ever seen. In fact, this was the mecca of what every cult leader probably had ever envisioned.

With the surrounding forest, it was hard to tell where our adjacent wall ended. Thinking back to when I jumped from the train to escape, I know it was just desert. There were no other smells and Reynard brought me to the front gate.

With this massive of forest, could there be a desert on the other side? Everywhere I looked was just forest pine trees as the sky painted a picture of forbidden nature, it was beautiful and yet intimidating.

Many men and women worked at the farmhouse. As we walked along outside the perimeter, Mother talked about what animals were here. The livestock of horses, cows, lambs, goats, pigs, chickens, and a rooster.

The women in the group were wide eyed and eager with joy. I could read it on their faces.

Some horses trotted over to be pet and sniff at the new smells. So many hands went out to pet the horses. Mother was winning their hearts with smiles and laughter. Mimicking the same joy as everyone else. I was digesting the scene, the surroundings, the people glancing in our direction. Their good natured, carefree attitudes portrayed a stress free life style.

This painted what Mother and his Grace wanted us to see. This was what they wanted to promise us. It was well intended, good-natured living, but why?

Nestled on the North side of the farm house, a long rectangular medical building was near the size of the green house. A giant Red Cross was carved on the front of the building.

North of the medical building, were the section of smaller cabins and many of them scattered around in groups.

"Once we place you in your living quarters and set you on a path where you earn your keep, you and your husband—"

Mother's voice drowned out around me as the women immediately whispered among one another. Many were shaking their heads, getting nervous at the thought of who their husband would be. Mother cleared her throat and asked us to be calm.

"Ladies, did you think you would be paired with a someone who wouldn't respect or value you?"

Women glanced at one another and didn't know how to answer.

"The answer is no. You are paired by the information we have on you and the questionnaire you took before coming here."

I leaned to Amara. "You filled out a questionnaire?"

The light bulb went off in Amara's eyes. She looked to have a complete understanding.

"I know how we were chosen." Amara said.

Mother was talking to the group as the nervous questions arise in the voices around her. I drowned them all out, looking beyond the group of women as my feet carried me a few steps north to see what was looking like my future.

At the forefront, there were men dressed the same as every other man with the large cotton shirts, deep v-necks and rolled up sleeves. They were all meant to be alike, just like us women. Some of the shirts were a cream, or a light brown like the women had different colored skirts.

The sound of a saw cutting into the lumber. The man sitting on a roof with each leg stretched on either side of the shingles as he nailed them in. The hauling of bringing up one side of a house and working together. They began to pause in their work as all of us women came down.

My mind immediately went to Zak. Reynard told me he was ok, but was he here? I couldn't really point him out in a crowd if I wanted to. I don't know his face and he doesn't know mine. Only the sound of our voices and even so, I don't think I could distinguish it from a group of men.

I wondered if he was a Watchmen and we crossed paths and didn't know it. At times, I wondered if I was to see him again.

The women around me stirred with crossed arms and hard expressions toward Mother. They were not happy about the thought of being courted. The shaking of their heads, whispers back and forth, Mother could see she was loosing the higher ground.

When I looked back, Hunter's eyes were on me. The knot in my throat formed, my mouth went dry. The knot in my stomach formed and I could have sworn my ovaries shriveled. I closed my eyes to remain calm and not allow him to think I feared him.

"Some of you might and that is up to his Grace for the decision." Mother said. "We all have much to learn and soon will be introduced and you all will be courted. This new life is to dip your toes into the water, not toss you into the roaring rapids."

Mother made it a point to be the reassurance they needed.

"Ladies..."

She picked up her skirts and slowly made her way through the crowd and stood in the middle. Her soothing and soft demeanor was no threat, it helped calm the rest of the ladies down.

"I assure you, his Grace has done extensive research into your backgrounds to pair you with a perfect match. We believe in unity and love. You all have suffered in your past lives, that stopped the moment your feet touched this dirt inside these walls."

I had to give it to Mother, she was reassuring with her

words. I carefully watched her growing fan club, as their eyes softened and inhaling her words as a gift for their ears to be blessed to listen to. I viewed this as manipulation. By making everyone believe what they had outside these walls was so terrible, like it wasn't worth fighting for. I bit my tongue, for now. I had a lot of work to do and hopefully get more people on my side.

OBSERVATION

After Mother was able to calm the rest of the group down. She wanted us to take a tour of the medical building. Hunter and Wallace held the doors open. Even in the middle of women, I hated that I looked up and caught Hunter's eyes on me. He winked, and the cold cement of the floor in the medical building was more welcoming.

The smell of fresh lemon with a small scent of vinegar was in the air. My nose crinkled and made the tip of it tingle. A long line of sheets on other side broke up barriers of patient rooms. It was one large giant hanger and everyone could hear everything.

Toward the back of the building, rooms built in modern plywood with smooth squared off sections was where nurses would be to get supplies and surgeries could be performed.

The terrifying thought of not being near a hospital made me fold my arms across my chest. I didn't understand how any of this was legal?

Mother instructed us to stop and break us apart by standing on either side the aisle. Coming from one of the sheeted room taking notes on a tablet, a tall, thin man came around, greeted Mother with a kiss on the cheek and stood in the middle, between us.

"This is our wonderful Doctor Ferrarius." Mother introduced. "He believes in herbal remedies, is a surgeon and educates the staff to become nurses and doctors."

Amara sucked up a short breath. The excitement in her energy and eager eyes to listen almost brought a smile to her face.

"Thank you Mother." His slight German accent was still noticeable to our ears. "Ladies, I am humbled to be here. We will thrive and live a modest life."

He paced down one side, looking into our eyes as he spoke. "We cannot ignore how modern medicine and technology brought us to where we are today. This building is state of ze art. We don't worry about dying over simple colds or flus."

He stopped in front of Amara and I. His thin long oval face, thick dark brown eyebrows and large deep brown eyes gave him a kindness and gentle demeanor. He wore what looked like a permanent five o'clock shadow. His sleek posture and tall stature was a man of intelligence, probably the God complex from what I have seen portrayed on television.

It was how he stopped and spoke to me and Amara that was nearly intoxicating. I could feel my hands sweat.

Doctor Ferrarius continued. "We will not starve, or suffer. Surgeries will be performed, broken bones mended and healed."

He spun on his heels. "I promise to you all, that I will be honest." He held his hands up to his lips in a prayer. "I will do what it takes and make the tough decisions." He began his stride on the other side. "His Grace has given me a fresh start at this new life, I will not disappoint."

I leaned over to Amara. "I can't tell if that's a good or bad thing."

His sharp features were striking to me. His smooth accent was a weakness of mine as I was a sucker for European accents. I wasn't the only one amongst us.

LUNCH WAS BACK in the dining hall. Our cold, dried feet from the thin air were starting to crack. It made it rough to stand in line. What got me through was knowing food was close by. My stomach growled as I haven't exerted myself like that in a long time. The other faces in the room wore like mine. Exhausted from the walk and digesting the information made all of us mentally weary.

My body relaxed sitting on the long hard bench. It was nice to get off my feet. I haven't felt that kind of fatigued since I tried and failed when I signed up at my local gym.

I wanted to get in shape and had never done strenuous exercise. One of the school teachers was a fitness nut and got eight of us to sign up as she would be a part time instructor. From burpees, to grueling sit ups and bench presses. Her daily circuit was intense for body building.

Even opening my eye lids was painful and Brant found humor in me trying to work out and tone myself.

"Just do a lot of cardio and more protein. That's all you need." He pointed out.

At times, it bothered me he wasn't a motivator. He just allowed me to fail, knowing the next week I didn't want to go back. He was never encouraging, just poked fun at my mistakes.

In the ready line, we could grab one chicken thigh, scoop sliced carrots, broccoli and bits of cauliflower, last was a scoop of diced potatoes.

The garlic and rosemary of food smelled divine. My two

prong fork picked up the diced potatoes first and I moaned in satisfaction. My mouth chewed the soft and yet crisp onion flavor of the potato, then salivated for more.

My eager hands picked up the piece of chicken and took big bites. I chewed slowly to savor every bit I could. Others were talking around me and all I wanted to do was eat and enjoy.

Yasmin, Esther and Amara were shocked and waited for me to take a breath before they started, but there was no stopping me. My body needed and painfully wanted each bite.

Realizing no one was talking anymore, when my eyes glanced up from my plate having about four bites left, I swallowed and became uncomfortable at my behavior.

"Sorry."

I sat straight up and fought with the urge not to shovel the food into my mouth.

"Do you guys remember going to a convention and filling out a form at a yellow tent with a virtual tour?" Amara asked the twins.

Yasmin and Esther both nodded.

"It's got to be that." Amara said.

"What?" Esther asked.

Amara leaned back in. "So did I. About a few years ago. That's how I won my trip. I simply answered personal questions about myself, my living situation, how I feel about certain things about life, my upbringing—"

"Sounds really personal." I interrupted.

I had never heard of such a questionnaire to wine a trip. I felt it was a true violation of privacy. Especially now a days where everything could be leaked on the internet.

"Exactly." Amara said. "I was at a low point in my life where I was done with everything and everyone. But the last question, I'll never forget."

"If you had to live your life over, would you?" Yasmin answered.

Her and Esther's expression was the same Amara had when we were on our tour. The lightbulb had gone off in their mind. Their shoulders sunk, their eyes turn downward.

AT NIGHT, it was the first time we were allowed to hang out before bed and talk down stairs, or stand outside in the fresh air near the woman's tower.

I stood on the loft in my nightgown observing from a far the women who were growing comfortable with their daily routine. They sat around the fire, joked about the men they saw and teased others.

Others stood near the book shelves or sat in the other couches making small talk. The chatter of all the voices was hard to concentrate on topics of discussion. The fire was lit below to keep our tower warm.

Our matching cream colored nightgowns was soft to the touch and kept me cozy. Amara came up to me and leaned her head on my shoulder.

"Want to know the topic of tonight?"

She seemed bored, from what I gathered by the annoyance in her tone.

"Let me guess. Our future betrothals?" I said in a French accent.

"Oh no, please…never again." She withheld a laughter.

Amara's sarcasm was my kind of cup of tea.

"Do you think the Watchmen are allowed to court us ladies?" She followed my cue trying to portray a voice from the 50s.

My eyes rolled. "Oh, please. You are really hung up on Reynard, aren't you?"

Quickly she play slapped my arm.

"Shhhh..."

Her eyes widened, turning her head from side to side making sure no one else heard us. The room was too noisy for any type of eaves droppers.

"I didn't say his name."

In an automatic response, I shrugged. "You didn't have to."

Amara tried to hide from her lips turning upward.

"Then, do you think they can pick for themselves?"

Her cute, yet shy demeanor made her almost girlish. Something was on her mind and she started to frown.

"What's wrong?"

"I'm sorry for not considering your feelings," she said. "You have a husband to think about and I'm here trying to brighten up the mood with talking about the good-looking men around here."

She was being considerate and I appreciated her for it. As a gentle gesture, I took one of her hands in mine.

"Your situation isn't like mine. I'm the one with the tough road ahead of me, not you. Don't feel bad."

"Alright ladies!" Mother projected her voice. "Time for your beauty sleep. Tomorrow we begin with handing out the schedules."

Mother turned her head and up in my direction where our eyes locked on one another. She stared at me like I was already a thorn on her side.

SHE'S BEEN FOUND

Brant was at the front desk of the hotel looking over the bill. He was being charged for the items that he forgot he ordered.

"Look, is there a manager I can speak to about these charges?" He pleaded. "I already have to go to another hotel because my credit card is maxed out from this place." He squinted as he read. "The couples massage, the daily breakfast cart and decorated champagne and chocolates, we…" He stopped himself. "I didn't get to use any of this."

The front desk clerk looked at him with pity in her eyes. He could sense she was aware of his situation. The police had been there a few nights prior to sweep the room and Liz's bags.

Brant was doing whatever it took to be cooperative. Looking at his three-thousand hotel bill was a stress he didn't need. Right now, he needed a win.

"Of course." She picked up her phone to speak low to someone that was behind the wall from where she was.

Brant thought he was mistaken as the tall and gangly

college student, Pat came from behind a door and approached the front desk clerk.

His mouth fell open as the young man didn't seem to recognize him in return.

"Pat?" Brant asked.

The young man's eyes shot up, smiled and shook his head. "Sorry, that's my twin. Sorry you met him." He continued to listen to the front desk clerk.

Brant noticed how obviously close this young man was to the front desk clerk. He was more relaxed and seemed more charismatic as he made her giggle with their hidden whispers of whatever the hell was between the two of them.

Taking a look at the name tag, Brant's eyes closed trying to have patience as his jaw flexed.

"Matt, is it?" Brant snapped. "Look, I don't think I should have to pay for these charges that I didn't use."

"But you pre-ordered them? Clearly right in our agreement, where you signed, it states there are no refunds."

The hard stare through Brant's eyes took everything in him not to reach over the counter and punch the kid in his arrogant face.

"Yes," Brant shaking from trying to stay calm. "I did preorder all of this, however—"

"Then, that's your confession." Matt was nonchalant.

The front desk clerk even tried to intervene knowing the difficult situation Brant was in.

Time was up for Brant's patience. Quickly, he reached over and grabbed the punk by the collar.

"My wife was kidnapped almost a week ago. I've been here searching for her."

He released his grip as the young man almost lost his footing. Brant pointed to the hotel bill.

"My wife and I were not able to use any of this because she disappeared the first day we were here."

Matt straightened out his shirt, and to Brant's surprise, he kept his cool.

"I heard about a guest we had here under those circumstances. I didn't know it was you. I apologize for my tone. I will get this taken care of."

Now, Brant felt like a jerk for grabbing the kid.

"Look, I'm sorry. I just haven't slept and—"

"Don't." Matt held up his hand. "My brother, Pat mentioned you two last night. He recognized her face on social media. He remembered you asking him where the restroom was."

Brant didn't expect someone like Pat to even think twice about remembering that fact.

"He did?"

"Pat feels bad. He said your wife seemed nice." Matt when to walk into the back office, he stopped at the door and turned around. "On the news, they said she was taken from the parking lot?"

To Brant, this was like reiterating the details over again to the police.

"On video it shows her going outside near the parking lot, but the other cameras outside were scheduled for maintenance, so we don't know exactly where she was taken."

Matt took in the information. It was clear there was something else, but he nodded and mentioned again he would take care of the bill.

"I've been calling you?" Detective Knight's sharp tone was behind Brant.

Brant slowly turned around seeing the detective with her hands in her pockets and resting-bitch-face attitude.

He patted his pants and felt foolish. "My cell phone must be in my rental car."

"I thought you were going to try and stay for a few more days?" She questioned.

"I'm checking out, well, trying to." Brant walked away from the counter.

The front desk clerk had heard enough drama of his.

"I can't afford this place any longer. I have to pick someplace else."

Detective Knight crossed her arms and bit her bottom lip to think of something.

"So what brings you by?"

Brant needed to move onto the next subject and not look weak, he hated to look weak in front of any woman, even at a time like this.

Detective Knight took a deep breath. "We found her. Her body was discovered earlier today."

The front desk clerk gasped with her hand over her mouth. Matt had come out from the back, saw the front desk clerk teary reaction and rushed over to console her.

The color from Brant's face dissipated. The hope in his heart drained like a puddle on the floor.

IN THE SEATTLE CITY MORGUE, Detective Knight stood with Brant and his brother-in-law, FBI agent, Julian Dermer. The Mortuary Attendant was already pulling the covered body out of temperature controlled container. Detective Knight and Julian were used to this scene and stood on both sides of Brant.

"When you're ready…" Detective Knight glanced over to Brant.

The red rim around his tired, stained eyes were deadened from the realization he was about to see his wife's dead body. The shock had not worn off and he stood frozen staring down at the sheet.

Julian cleared his throat. "We're ready." He maneuvered

his lips, building up the confidence to see his sister-in-law's body.

Carefully from the crown of the head, the Mortuary Attendant pulled down the sheet to expose the face, and collarbone, to softly fold down and lay on top of the chest above the breast. The indication of the autopsy stitches forked to touch each collarbone.

"Shit!" Julian took a step back, holding back the tears.

Brant studied the beautiful face had bruises and deep cuts on her cheek. Her eyes were kept closed. The ride side of her head was heavily bashed in from a blunt force of something.

"I'll give you some time." The Mortuary Attendant left the three of them.

With his hands at his hips, he continued to nod and stare at the corpse.

"That's her." Julian said.

Detective Knight watched Brant's reaction. He barely had one. Instead, he seemed to be taking a closer look.

"Detective..." Julian moved around Brant. "Where was the body discovered?"

"She was found behind the amphitheater wall, not far from the Chihuly Gardens," She kept her eye on Brant. "Where Mr. Thomas last saw her. She was about two-hundred and fifty yards."

Julian grabbed his cell phone and sighed. "I should call Shannon. The family needs to know."

"Brant, can you confirm this is your wife?" Detective Knight asked.

Watching the suspicion grow inside Brant, there was something not making sense.

"Detective!" Julian snapped. "Both of us are here and clearly he is distressed and I already confirmed—"

"It's not her." Brant said, staring at the body.

Julian spun around, baffled. "Clearly he won't accept—"

"It's not Liz." Brant pointed to the young woman's face. "See, no beauty mark on her face. I do recognize this woman though."

"You do?"

Detective Knight and Julian looked at one another confused.

"I saw her on the day Liz disappeared." Brant recalled, "for a split second I thought this woman was my wife. Not only did their faces match, but in a way, so did their clothes. When I found Liz, I made a joke I found her doppelgänger."

MARBLE COMPASS

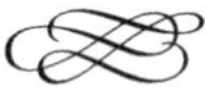

When the rooster crowed in the morning from the speakers in our room. I wasn't startled like before. It had been a pleasant welcoming to another morning in the last few days. The first thing I saw now, was my carved names of my family members. I worked on it each night adding more. My fingers tracing names each morning. Today, Brant was the first name I saw.

Heading down the stairs, dressed and ready for the day. It was a nice feeling we didn't have to be herded like cattle. We all knew where the dining hall was and went we were ready.

Today was scrambled eggs, rolled sausage and a small bite of wheat bread. The food was a warm and pleasant smell that reminded of when I would make Sunday breakfast at home. The boys always wanted pancakes with a hint of vanilla. They loved sausage and hated bacon.

Brant would joke they must not be American because bacon was an staple in our house. Brant's taunting made them gullible.

"You know, one day they are going to be able to give it back to you." I warned from the kitchen.

The same happened to my sister and I. Our father always taunted us with humor and then before I knew it, we were sharper, quick witted and faster than him.

It was moments I remembered that brought my mood up. No one would be able to change the loving memories of my family. Last night, I agreed to myself that I would remember one good memory each day. I was being my own therapist at this point. Which might help, or in times of darkness, it could hinder me.

Seeing the eggs and then the sausage. I thought about the sweet pigs I saw grunting and rolling in the mud on the farm yesterday. My stomach rumbled because my body craved the delicious meat. Seeing the pigs yesterday gave me a touch of guilt.

The freshly squeezed orange juice was served in our pewter cups. This had to have been my favorite burst of flavor so far. I had never tasted anything so crisp and fresh in all my life.

"You'll need your strength." Amara said.

I poked my sausage and took a bite and couldn't help but roll my eyes.

"I hate that babe taste so good." I chewed.

Mother strolled in on her heels with a big bright smile, her big white hair in a thick French braid off to one side. Her royal blue dress robes with silver thread of the floral decor shimmered in the natural light.

"Good morning ladies."

Her voice had a chime to it. She carried a portable chest in her hands.

"Welcome to Monday."

Thinking back to my birthday being on a Sunday, Monday was the tour and I was kidnapped. I know I have been here for three nights already. That meant Zak and I were in the van and then in the train for four days.

Knowing it had been a little over a week, I lost my appetite. I pushed my plate in front of me.

"When you are done with breakfast. Please come see my on stage and I will hand you your schedules." Mother set the portable chest on her table.

I was the first to stand up and dispose the food on my plate. Next, I set the plate and fork through the side doors of the conveyer belt.

I carefully walked up the steps and across the stage as all eyes seemed to be on me. I stood at the front of Mother's table.

"Good morning Liz." Mother greeted.

I gave her a flicker of a faint smile. She didn't even bother opening the chest.

"For now. I will have you in my study room until you meet with Aldrich."

"Who's he?" I asked.

"Someone who is qualified to place you."

Mother was ready to move onto the next woman standing behind me, but I didn't give up so easily.

"Why can't I tell you? I'm an adult, it's like going for a review, right?"

Mother's nails tapped on her table. "No, it's not that simple."

"Then, let's make it that simple."

Mother glanced around me and gave a slight nod to a Watchmen. I turned to see Reynard not pleased to have to deal with me.

"Yes, Mother." Reynard asked.

Mother paused, staring up at me. Then, she gave the order. "Take her."

Before Reynard could grab me by the arm, I bent down to get a closer look at Mother.

"Funny, you want us to feel free, but we can't even share our own thoughts."

Reynard gripped my arm and I didn't fight back. I allowed him to walk me off the stage and out of the dining hall.

Amara and the twins were horrified to watch me leave. A part of me was scared, because I had no idea where I was going.

I WAS surprised I didn't travel far. Reynard and I went around the corner and into a study room. He shoved me inside.

"You're trying to cause trouble." He closed the door and stood guard in front of it.

The room was about halfway done. There was still a shelving space to fill and paintings sat on the floor covered in sheets. There was no furniture in the room, very stuffy and unkept.

"Why would I do that?" I remarked.

Reynard shook his head. "Don't play games. I told you something in confidence, remember. I'm not suppose to speak about him to you.

He was talking about Zak. I dropped the tough woman attitude because I wanted to know more.

"Alright, I'm sorry." I pleaded. "How is he?"

Taking in a deep breath, I could see Reynard found it tough not to answer me.

"He's not causing trouble, like you."

Me feet felt the grime dust of the room at the bottom of my feet. The marble floor underneath me was a cream and dark brown design. When I stood back to see it clearly, I saw in the marble resembled of a compass.

"He's thought of everything, hasn't he?"

I felt I was terrible at direction, but when I thought about the lay of the land from my tour, I had been spot on with my sense of direction. This was another moment, Brant would have been proud of me, because in Los Angeles, I was always turned around.

"You don't see it yet, but his Grace is a good man." Reynard said.

I pressed my lips together and stared up in the matching ceiling. The peaked view of the sky and hand painted design matching the floor was unique.

"What if I never see it?" I said.

Reynard and I looked at one another. I read the disappointment on his face. Both of us were interrupted when Mother tried to come into the room, but Reynard blocked the door.

Mother exhaled as she came in, only speaking to me.

"Why?" Her arms outwardly. "Liz, I know you hate your situation, but what you said to me, I can't have that in there."

"My situation?" I asked.

How this woman acted as though I was a defiant child at school was making my blood boil.

Mother was trying to keep her tone calm. She paced the room with her hands pressed together up to her lips. She paused and stood a few feet away from me, directly in my line of sight.

"I have to remind myself you are not like the others. I know you have something worth fighting for outside these walls." She dropped her hands to clasp at her stomach. "Frankly, I'm jealous."

I could feel my ears burn and turn red. When she began to take a step toward me, I stepped back. The last thing I needed from her was comfort.

"Don't pretend with me." I gritted. "You and his Grace are going to use me for something."

Mother turned to Reynard. “Could you please leave us.”

Reynard and I gave one another a glance, when his eyes returned to Mother, he nodded and left the room.

Her beautiful styled hair turned back in my direction. She took one step forward and this time I didn’t move. I knew she wanted our words to stay between us.

“You’re right. We want to use you. You might be the success story we need.”

I wasn’t following along. “Don’t keep me in suspense.”

Mother took another, soft step in my direction. “I want to fix you.” Her eyes held back tears. “I suffer like you with the biocurrate uterus. Doctor Ferrarius was carefully selected and brought to fix me.”

A chill drifted into the room. Goosebumps formed from my ankles and spread up my legs and body. I was starting to understand why his Grace and Mother needed me.

“You want him to perform the surgery on me first.” I stated.

Mother pointed to the tip of her nose. “You’re smart.” She whispered.

“If he’s successful, then he performs on you?” The confusing conversation I felt was not lining up. “I don’t understand what you would want from me?”

Mother put her pressed hands together at her lips as she took another step toward me. We were not less than six inches away. I felt the desperation from her body and saw the sadness in her eyes. This was difficult for her to ask, or a painful reminder of what she couldn’t do.

“I’ve had brilliant surgeons tell me my condition is not fixable. If you’re a candidate and the surgery is successful. I will have made you feel whole.”

A single tear dropped from my eye. I quickly wiped it away. I hated how this was the bond between us and somehow she knew how I felt.

"If Doctor Ferrarius is not successful with me, I want you to stay long enough to have a child, for me."

The blood drained from my ears. I didn't think I heard her right.

"Me, have your baby?"

She nodded. "Think of it." She grabbed and held my hands with her cold, thin fingers and squeezed. "I give you a gift and you can go out and have as many children as you want. All I want is one."

"Go out, meaning..."

"If I can't have the surgery and you agree to hand me over your first born. I will help you escape and return you back to your husband and children."

Her words were a strange tune to my ears. Another tear fell from my eye, but this time I didn't wipe it away. I was happy, hopeful and yet confused. I stopped myself and realized one problem.

"What if both surgeries are successful?"

Mother wiped my tear off my face. "You agreeing, no matter the cost is your ticket to freedom. If I can bare my own children, I will still make sure to set you free."

It was a wonderful thought, but it meant I would have months, or over a year. Mentally I wasn't sure if I could be stable enough to go through with all of this.

"What about his Grace? He won't let me go easily."

Mother shook her head. "You don't worry about him. This one is our secret."

Her words felt genuine. The desperate part of me wanted to agree right away and see where it would take me. I hesitated because I still didn't know how to trust her.

"Don't answer right away." She said. "Let me take you to sewing to distract you and think about it. Come to me when you are ready to give your answer."

GREEN PILLOW

I followed Mother across the grass and up toward the sewing cabin.

"Since everyone else has their instructions. I figure you could start here today and you and I will see each other later."

Mother held onto my arms and pulled me in for a hug. My arms at my sides, I could see she thought me following her was a sign I already agreed.

"Good luck."

Mother turned me toward the cabin, and like a mother releasing her toddler on the first day of school, she gave me a little shove in the right direction.

I didn't have the fastest pace, I was still trying to digest her offer. I could have the surgery I had been researching for the past few years and it would be at no cost. If I remembered correctly, it was a six to eight weeks of recovery. With the stress of my surgery, I might have to take certain hormones and give myself shots.

Then, after a month of that, I now needed to know who was going to be the father. Did she just need me to be the carrier, or the egg donor? Or both? Would I have to sleep with his Grace? Could I handle giving up my own child?

I opened the door to a classroom full of women sitting at long bench tables and sewing kits sitting in front of them.

The rounded woman who gave me the dirty look was at the front of the class. When she saw me, she sighed.

"In or out?" She shouted in my direction with a thick New York accent.

Lost in my own thoughts, I didn't realize I was keeping the door open.

"Sorry." I closed it and made my way over to sit in the back.Adjusting my skirts as they snagged on the wooden benches, I sat near the aisle. I preferred quick escapes if I must.

"I have never picked up a needle and thread. Never had to where I came from," the woman to my right said.

She was nervous and I could see she chewed on her finger nails. They were blistered and bloody already and it was just day one.

My hand reached out to settle on top of hers. "We will get through this."

Naturally the sympathetic teacher in me came out. She settled in and thanked me. The young woman put her hands on her lap and straightened her posture.

The woman in charge instructed us to pick up the needle and thread through the tip and have half the string go through. This was where my stress would come into play. I was a woman of patience, but threading string through a tiny piece at the tip of the needle was not easy for me to do. I kept bumping and bend the thread. Other women around me touched the tip of the thread onto their tongue, then with their thumb and index finger they rolled it to a point.

I tried and failed. This was why my grandmother did it for me. It took me twice as long as my sister Shannon was almost done with her first stitching. A gentle hand reached over to take my needle and thread. The woman on my right put the thread through with ease.

"Now I have made you feel better." She quipped.

I smiled back. "You certainly did."

The blonde woman from the front was passing out square patterns in different colors. When she approached me at the end, her pear shape, fuller face and rounded cheeks waited for my answer without even asking.

There was one satin green one left. I pointed to it and she pulled it from the middle and flopped it on the desk. The color made me smile and think of the boys. They both liked green and fought about it most of the time. When I shared they could like different shades of green, I smiled to the thought they looked at me like I was the crazy one, because to them there was only one shade of green to like.

"We will start with pillows first. Then, baby clothes and so on. If you are wicked enough with a needle, you can help me with the design of dresses."

Me and the woman next to me seemed to be the only ones in the class with an unsure expression. When we looked at one another, we couldn't help but giggle.

AS I BENT my fingers to close into fists, the stiffness of my fingers felt bruised. My skin was dry, cracked and I was nearly done. My ring indentation was in the stages of plumping out, like I never had a wedding ring and band before. I still carried the slight discoloration, but I didn't want my indention to leave me.

When it was announced we were done for the day, my hands had never felt happier. Retracting and expanding my fingers was an ache I had never felt. My grandmother was right. My generation was lucky to have sewing machines. We left our pillows on our seats and formed in a single file line to walk out and down the stairs.

Standing at the door, the woman who was teaching the course held in one hand a pin cushion. Before we left, she asked each of us to put the needle in the cushion. When I pushed my pin in, I could feel the stiff cotton as the needle slid into it's new home.

I didn't realize how much humidity was in the air until I stepped onto the porch. Since the linen press and laundry was next door, the humidity drifted by in a thick wave that seemed to hover. The instant moisture struck my face. The rich earthy sweet smell with the pine forest was a fresh scent that was new to my senses.

The barn doors were opened wide to the linen area. Everyone looked miserable and sweating. I was thankful Mother did have me go here today.

Halfway down the hill, the woman who taught the class rushed to my side nearly out of breath. She gripped my forearm. When she saw her grip, she apologized and then put on a fake smile and tucked her hair behind her ears.

"Can we talk?"

Four other women I had never seen before gathered around. I was uncomfortable, but I didn't feel threatened.

"This way." The woman tilted her head toward the back of the building. "It's safe there."

"Make this quick," I told them. "You know he has cameras all around."

The woman stood with her arms crossed over her large chest. She stood angled as one hip popped out. Then, she stuck out her hand.

"I'm Angela." We shook hands. "We just need to know. You the woman who was not supposed to be here?"

Stunned, I didn't even think my presence mattered.

"Yes, that is true." I answered.

Angela and the other women were shaking their heads and hissed at the idea.

"Rumor has it that you traveled with a male?"

Angela was eager to hear. I felt all of their eyes weighed heavily on me. It was a suffocating feeling. I wasn't sure if sharing was the dumbest or smartest idea.

"Back off you snow birds!" Angela's accent was thick as she waved her arms around. Apologies all around, the women stepped back.

"Sorry. It's been drid lately."

"I'm sorry?" I was confused by her context.

"Sorry, we're annoyed. I know we come off a bit strong. Trying to decompress after living in a big city isn't an easy attitude to turn off."

"Was he, one of them?" Another woman with dark hair and illuminating blue eyes transfixed on me.

I had never seen someone so delicate and yet so scary to see because of the brightness in her eyes.

"One of them?" I was confused.

"A Watchmen?" Angela asked.

"I don't think so. He tried to find ways to escape. So, I doubt it." I answered.

"Did you ever get a look at him?" Angela asked.

I shook my head. Angela smacked her tongue against her teeth in annoyance. She took a small step forward. Her big round baby blue eyes shined now and stared into mine.

"Was he good to you?"

"If you're hinting if he was inappropriate, the answer is no."

My head spun around as they they all exhaled.

"Word has gotten around Hunter has taken a liking to you." Angela said.

Her words went through me like a winter's wind. It chilled me the second it pierced my ears. I stayed silent, my eyes looking down. I didn't know their angel and wasn't comfortable knowing where they stood.

"Hey..." Angela touched one of my shoulders. "He's a creep. Do us a favor? Don't take him on yourself. You need something, ask."

I nodded and deep down. I was thankful for the support.

"Why are you not supposed to be here?" She asked.

Thinking back, I was never informed if I was allowed to tell anyone. At this point, I didn't know who they reported to, so I couldn't sound desperate, or angry.

"Classic case of mistaken identity. I resembled the woman and the kidnapers got the wrong woman."

"I told you." One woman said.

"I want you to understand sump tin. Life here is a hell of a lot easier." Angela pointed to the ground. "We are Faithfuls to his Grace. We believe in this place and we don't want trouble."

"I don't either." I put my hands up in defense.

Angela and the others seemed to silently agree with nodding their heads.

"You're a good person." Angela tapped her fingers on one side of her hip. "Us women, we have to stick together."

When she walked away from me, she brushed by me, barely grazing my shoulder. She was a tall and thick woman with good child-barring hips. If she wanted to shoulder check me, she would have.

WHITE ROOM

When I came around the corner. Mother stood on the grounds with her hands folded in the creases of her elbows. She was in the same spot where she left me earlier, before sending me off to sewing. Her eyes watching Angela and the other women as they chatted and walked down the slope without a care in the world.

"She's an intimidating woman." Mother's eyebrows raised in Angela's direction.

I exhaled heavily. She didn't need to remind me.

"Was she at least kind?"

I nodded. "She was. She also wanted to know if I was the one who traveled with a man, and asked if he was kind to me." I paused, pressing my lips together.

The silence fell between us, Mother turned her head slightly, watching me as I stayed quiet.

"Was he?"

"Of course. It's not him. It's…"

Inside, I hesitated on how I should answer. A part of me, and a big part felt uneasy about explaining my few interactions with Hunter. I wasn't sure if I could trust her. They both were here long before me.

A swift change in the wind caught us both by surprise as the trees swayed, resulting in the pine needles brushing against neighboring trees and the loud creek in their trunks made us pause to watch.

The sight was unreal to me. I didn't grow up around a lot of trees, but with the wind and watching them sway. I would easily want to run inside and believe they were going to come crashing down. Then, the wind faded. I couldn't help but stay in place, watch our surroundings as the pine trees swayed, as if nature was trying to give me some sort of a sign.

When my eyes drifted down to glance at Mother's face. It was the sparkle of interest in her eyes. It was short lived. I stiffened, because looking beyond, behind her, Hunter peeled himself off from around the cabin wall, heading in our direction. His cold blue eyes fixed on mine, staring intently. Even with the sun beating down behind me, his presence made the blood in my body run cold.

"It's nothing." I whispered with tight lips.

When Hunter looked at me, I felt as though he wanted my soul. A corner of his lip turned upward and made the vile in the back of my throat rise.

"Something I need you to do. Follow me." Mother picked up her skirts.

Hunter suggested I go next, I tightened my frame and picked up my skirts to follow Mother as we were heading in the direction of the windmill.

Up the slope on the higher ground, Mother waited for Hunter to rush ahead and open the door for us.

"Stay down here." She ordered him.

The disappointed, sour face he made as I closed the door behind me was priceless. I headed up the tight spiral staircase. Three stories with heavy skirts, thin air and mixed emotions from today. I breathed heavily wishing I had fallen through with my gym days.

At the top of the stairs was a dark stained wood door with black iron bolts, was hard to see. The few LED lights carved in the stone walls up the stairs didn't give much light. Mother knocked a few times with her delicate touch. When the door opened, the glow of bright white shined behind the man.

A man to be nearly forty answered with a warm smile and welcoming face. His high forehead and angular edges was quite symmetrical. His jaw was more squared off with deep sunken blue eyes, his short blonde hair and receding hairline showed his age, but the clean shaven face gave him a youthful glow.

He welcomed Mother with a kiss on the cheek, pleased to see her. When he saw me, his eyes brightened.

"This must be Elizabeth. Our mistaken traveler. Please, everyone, welcome."

He greeted us in and I bitterly followed suit.

The three-hundred and sixty five panoramic view was breathtakingly beautiful. His home on the inside was furnished with modern furniture, everything was white besides the trim of the many televisions taking up one side of the wall.

"My apologies." Mother whispered to me. "There was no other guard around at the time."

I didn't say anything back to her. My eyes scanned the elevated view just above the clouds. The heavenly view of being three stories at the highest point, and gape over the grounds, took my breath away. Seeing the castle nearly in full view, instead of looking up to it, and the village and farm with a birds eye perspective. Something about this windmill made everything else look peaceful.

Hundreds of monitors flipping images from live camera feeds. He had eyes on everyone. My wandering curiosity had me watch the grounds to the castle, to the interior of the the dining hall. People in the study and other common areas Nearly every inch of the grounds in and out had some sort of live feed.

I didn't see cameras in sleeping quarters, restrooms and showers. At least there was a small amount of privacy even though, I felt sure there was some sort of listening device.

There was a small glass coffee table in the middle of the room with two couches. Mother directed me to sit on one side as the man sat on the other.

"Elizabeth, welcome." He greeted me with a big smile.

Mother cleared her throat. "This is Aldrich. The man who will have you answer some questions."

Aldrich reached out and extended his hand. I took it and gave him a firm grip.

"Ouch!" Aldrich pulled his hand back. "This mishap is feisty."

"Mishap? Stealing me away from my husband and family was a mishap?" I snickered.

"Elizabeth." Aldrich trying to give me an authoritive tone.

"My name is, Liz!" I quipped.

"Of course." He corrected himself. "Liz, since his Grace has decided to keep you among us. There are a series of questions I will need you to answer and be honest. Are you up for it?"

"Not really, but what choice do I have." My arms crossed.

My body wanted to sink into the comfortable cushion on the white couch. If I didn't wan't to be rude, I would slouch. I hated how his comfortable couch felt like it wanted to hug me at all angles, my muscles were able to relax.

Aldrich smacked his knees as he stood. He walked over to

his monitor station and grabbed a tablet. He fumbled around as he walked back to hand it to me.

"Liz, I'm not the person who decides your fate. His Grace has worked tirelessly for our Faithful way. How you answer, his althorigum computes who you should be paired with."

"There are no wrong answers. Just know that. I know you don't trust us. But understand, you're not going home. We need to make the most out of this new life for you."

I glanced over at Mother, she gave me a sideways glance with a hidden smile as she stood to give me space. In the back of my mind, recalling our conversation earlier, I was still contemplating whether or not I was ready to go along with the corrective surgery. It weighed heavily on me, because I was not sure if I could have someone else's baby, or hand off one of my own.

My California driver's license picture was the first image I saw. My big smile, baby blue background and a slight tan on me made the white in my eyes and teeth stand out.

"On the side are the different questions." Aldrich pointed down on the screen. "When you have completed a set, it will turn green and you are prompt to select the next."

I'm not an idiot with technology!

There were no wrong answers, but if I wanted to be someone else, that could mean these answers could pair me with someone I didn't get along with, or have nothing in common.

Thinking about my answers. I selected the first top button to answer about my childhood, the schools I went to and how was my upbringing.

Regardless, if I was set up with a suitor, that meant I would have to break my marriage vows. Be in someone else's bed. What if I ended up with someone who didn't care? If I went with Mother's plan, would this person be ok with my choice? Either way, it was my golden ticket, but that could be over a year from now.

My clothes suddenly gave me an itch on my chest. I heard Mother and Aldrich in the background talking and I chose not to listen as the blood rushed through my ears. My eyes stared at the screen, my fingertips hovering over the screen's keyboard. Answering honestly or dishonestly came down to, the decision of how I wanted to continue my future here. What person did I want to be?

The tablet rested on my legs. Holding my head up as my fingers rubbed my forehead. I put myself in a crazy situation that I didn't think I could back out from.

The front door closed behind me, I spun to see Aldrich put his hands in his pockets, as he swiftly turned to make his way on the light brown hardwood floor in my direction. The buzzing of the monitors and the heels of his dress shoes echoed in my mind.

Slowly my eyes looked up to see him at a distance in his blue eyes showing me empathy. He was sad about something.

Before he parted his lips, I began to plead my case. My fingers hovering over the tablet.

"I am of no use to his Grace, I cannot bare children."

Aldrich eyebrows raised. "Wise observation."

He sat across from me with one ankle resting on his other knee. He rested his elbow on the arm of the couch and then to his face.

My sore fingers wanted to continue, but they pulsed and throbbed from the sewing class earlier. I pumped both hands to stretch them out. I winced as the pain stretched from palms to the tips of my fingers. Every muscle throbbed. The pulse in my wrists beat harder and the blood flow sent sharp pains of numbness to the tips of my fingers.

"Do you want to discuss your condition?" He asked.

My eyes lifted from the tablet. He put his hands up in

defense, immediately recognizing the wrong questions to be asked.

"Just trying to help."

I stared at the information that was to be filled out. They needed my current address, social security number, and continued marital information.

"Why do I have to fill all of this in? Once you run my social, you'll be able to pull whatever you want."

Aldrich's fingers tapped on the arm of his chair.

"True. Just answer to appease me."

I typed in my social security number. At this point, between my drivers license and school credentials, it was obvious he could get whatever information he wanted. If I lie, it meant that he could point it out later, it wouldn't do anything by prolong the mistrust they would have in me.

What I needed was to placate my situation. I just wasn't sure if that meant to go along with Mother's plan.

VODKA

The air in the room was stuffy. All the monitors and technology made the air dry and warm. I coughed to clear my throat.

"Where are my manors!"

Aldrich bounced up from the couch. He rushed over to his simplistic modern all white kitchen. He opened up cabinets to look for something.

I envied his flushed cabinets with the sleek and smooth surface. Everything about him screamed simplistic and minimalistic. He opened what I thought was a cabinet drawer, ending up being the refrigerator. My eyes widen being intrigued.

He grabbed a pitcher of lemon water and poured into two blue goblets. On a tray, he grabbed an old blue decanter of something and poured into two shot glasses.

"Might help you relax."

He brought the tray over and set it on the coffee table. He handed me a shot of something.

I made the mistake of putting my nose close to the rim of

the shot glass. The intense smell of vodka, or as I joked with Brant, gasoline. My nose crinkled. *God! I wish he had wine.*

The shot glass was held up by my thumb, index and middle finger. My eyes staring at the clear liquid in the small mini goblet. The temptation could help ease my mind, that was a nice thought. After everything I have endured, I told myself I deserved this.

"Too many bad nights in college with this old friend." I toasted and shot back in one gulp.

The smooth liquid glided down my throat in ease. I felt it travel down to my stomach and spread its warmth and the heat from my cheeks and ears as I flushed. As usual, my face puckered for a second, but it helped take the edge off.

Looking down at the tablet, there was a sense of ease as I answered the questions. With one shot down, I was already feeling a touch tipsy.

"Aldrich, what if there are questions I don't want to answer?"

His index finger traced the rim of the shot glass. In no hesitation, he wanted to crack a smile answering without fail. "Your process will move slowly. You'll probably be assigned duties away from other women. I know you'll never reconnect with Zak."

My body sat up in reaction to Zak's name. Aldrich folded one ankle over the other knee again. He knew something, I could tell how he stared at me.

"Zak was my travel companion." I admitted.

He nodded, reached over and grabbed a glass of lemon water and took a sip.

"He's asked about you."

I swallowed the lump in my throat. I needed to be of sound and mind and not share what Reynard has shared with me.

"How is he?" My voice croaked.

"Thriving. He's very happy here, but still asks about you."

I reached down and took the second glass of lemon water. My lips touched the rim of the glass. The lemon was a burst of sour and citrus that dried in taste. The cool sensation of the refreshing water should quench my thirst, but I felt it dry instantly as it traveled down my throat.

The sudden idea came to me as my fingers hovered. My brother-in-law is an FBI agent. With my disappearance, he would have to run a trace of my credit cards, social security and driver's license. If anyone besides the police departments was inquiring about me, this should send up a red flag.

This could have been the vodka talking through me, but with the old help of liquid courage, I decided to play them at their own game. I was answering honestly. In fact, the more information I could insight Aldrich with, it could help me in return. My brother-in-law had to have been helping Brant and the other police stations. Something should ping about my whereabouts in the scary technological world.

Aldrich came back over with the vodka decanter and poured two more shots. I giggled this time.

"How did you know alcohol makes people answer honestly." I felt my mouth move, my voice speak but I was having nearly an out of body experience, not being able to control one or the other.

My hands didn't even feel sore anymore. I reached down and shot back like it was water. The taste wasn't as bad this time, but I felt it rush down to my stomach and made me feel warmer.

Aldrich took the other shot. "I will give you space."

I smacked my lips and puckered them in concentration. I cradled the tablet with both hands staring at the screen. I was looking at questions, what I do for a living, how long I had been doing my job? Did I like my job? Did I have a degree? What college did I attend? Did I like college? What groups were I apart of?

A few minutes after that, the questionnaire continued to get personal. What people did I admire? Who are my influences? In my perspective how do I make others feel?

Aldrich reminded me, there were no wrong answers. It was based on personality matching. I felt like I was taking a psychological test all over again. In order to get my teaching credentials, taking a test like this shows someone's mental state during stress and their reactions.

The questions were daunting. Everything from my childhood, to my schools, college days, dating preference, how many partners and then socially, who was I as a person. Then it dove into my desires and interests.

"Jesus…" My elbows rested on my thighs reading off the tablet. "I can't believe people filled this out. Did you offer them vodka?"

"No." Aldrich chuckled. "I figured you were special and deserved it. Also, I am joining you because this journey hasn't been easy for me either."

Aldrich poured both of us another shot of vodka. His blotchy face and glazed eyes slumped before me on the glass coffee table. "Don't make this hard on yourself." I could hear the sincerity in his tone. "Accept this is your new life."

The beautiful sunset just above the clouds was a beautiful mixture of day and night. The stars making their appearance in the East, as the soft beautiful glow of blue and orange mixture of colors bleeding from one into the other on the West. I was witnessing the best view of what the world could offer.

I sipped my vodka this time. I wasn't sure how I was able to function. At this moment, I knew I was pretty much drunk. Fifty questions later, the tablet let me know I was on the last question:

If you could change your life, be someone else, leave everything behind with no consequences, would you?

In my current emotional state. Being kidnapped, forced into living in a new situation and told to forget my life. I couldn't answer this question. I tossed the tablet on the glass table. The 'clank!' Of the back of the tablet smacking the glass startled Aldrich.

My head shaking as he picked up the tablet, his eyes shot back at me with inquisition.

"I'm sorry, I can't answer the last question." I sat back to allow the comfy couch cradle me.

The smooth and quick move of his hand, the tablet spun effortlessly in my direction to see only to choose a *yes* or *no* answer.

"A scenario, you and I meet in a bar in Seattle." He began. "You just had an argument with your husband. I ask you this question randomly, what would be your response?"

I sprang up from the couch, nearly loosing my footing. This caught Aldrich off guard. My mind immediately went to the night Brant, and I argued once again about IVF treatment. The argument started at the restaurant, continued in the hotel bar, and then our hotel room.

"How could you have known that?"

With both hands raised in defense, Aldrich kept his calm demeanor.

"Liz…I didn't mean to upset you."

At this point, I would blame the multiple shots of vodka for my quick temper. Digesting the question. I jumped to the worst conclusion. I saw the toggle to choose from as Aldrich had the tablet still in the palm of his hand. *Yes* or *No?*

Fear draped over like a dark cloud. Would I have

answered yes, or would it be a sharp no? I was happy in my marriage and I loved the boys. Sure, where times tough? Of course! What marriage didn't have it's challenges.

My mind began to race and thanks to the vodka, my head was spinning a mile a minute and I wasn't making sense in my own head.

My last few ex-boyfriends popped in. They broke up with me because I couldn't carry their children. One of them was a successful and very wealthy businessman, surely he could afford any surgery I wanted.

No, Liz! Don't go there!

My face in my hands, I thought about my fight with Brant, and how stupid it was that money was the one thing holding me back from possibly carrying my own child.

I found the question to be unfair and it made me snap at Aldrich.

"I can't be honest right now! I have been kidnapped, ripped from my life. I don't know if I would change anything!"

I yelled in the palms of my hands.

The air in the room was stuffy. I could hear the humming of the monitors, the faint sound of the screens clicking over the next framed scene every few seconds. The alcohol was getting the better of me, and I was beginning to lose my temper. My hands clenched at my sides.

"That questionnaire is a joke. It doesn't know me, or tell you how I feel. How I am as a person." I seethed through my teeth.

"No, it doesn't." Aldrich agreed. "But your social media, online shopping and background tell me more."

"Liar!" I yelled. "Whatever this cult is, I don't want to be apart of it!"

I could feel my hands trembling, my body shaking from all the built up anger from being in this place.

"Don't you understand? None of you can convince me this life is better for me!"

I didn't think twice. I stormed to the door, opened it wide and stomped down as best as I could, still reeling from the effects of the alcohol.

WARM SHOWER

"Liz!" Aldrich's voice wasn't far behind.

He raced halfway down and touched my shoulder. I spun around.

"What?"

His gentle blue eyes pleaded with mine. "Let me help you. I can make the pain of not being able to have a child go away." He pressed his hands into a prayer. "We have the technology, we have the surgeon."

My bottom lip quivered. My eyes glossed over. He had no idea what Mother offered me. That decision still weighed on my heart of what to do. I shook my head.

"I want to go home, Aldrich. I want my husband and boys back."

Deflating before my eyes, he rested his body against the wall of the staircase. He put his hands in his pockets and hung his head.

"You know I can't make that happen. There is too much risk sending you back out."

I disagreed. "I can stay silent."

"You know his Grace won't risk it. I need you to learn to be on our side."

The lump in my throat was too painful to swallow.

"The missing hole in my heart will never go away. I can never be on your side for as long as you keep me away from my family. "

I felt a tear rolled down my cheek. Holding myself against the wall down the staircase, when I flung the door open, Hunter was standing at the doorway, waiting for my return. His thin lips turned upward. My vodka wanted to make a reappearance. I felt like an idiot for not remembering him.

"Shall I escort you back to your sleeping quarters, Liz?" His lips lingered on the *Z*, his eyes undressing me. "After you."

More than anything I wanted to melt into the floor. I didn't want to go anywhere with him.

When I didn't respond, his patience wore thin. He stepped toward me, inches from my face.

"Liz?" I heard the steps of Aldrich coming down. When he saw Hunter, I heard him sigh. "Please escort her back."

"With pleasure."

Hunter's stink of sour food from his breath made me want to gag. He yanked me by the arm and dragged me down the slope.

I pulled my arm out of his grip.

"Let me go!" I snapped.

This only seemed to have turned him on as his sly smile stretched across his face. This was a game to him. He rushed me, startling me. I wasn't at my best with the alcohol still consumed in my stomach.

The night had taken over, the castle was not far, but there wasn't enough lights to help guide me back. My vision blurred and it was harder to see as the crisp night and darkness was consuming and closing in and around me.

I stumbled, catching myself and struggling to stay upright. Hunter was a few paces back laughing.

"Slow down, do you even know where to go?"

His cackle angered me as my fists stayed at my side.

The rustling of the trees, crunching sounds of sticks, grass and leaves, made me dizzy to keep track of as I was trying to focus on my surroundings. I blinked constantly, then widen my eyes to help me focus.

He was right. In fact, I didn't know where I was. Now, I'm pissed at myself for not remembering.

My body stiffened when I heard Hunter clear his throat. Apparently reminding me that I was going the wrong way. He didn't even bother helping.

"My, my…Liz, have you been drinking?" Hunter laughed.

Disoriented from the slope and sense of direction. I thought I saw the sewing cabin or was it the black smith cabin? The cold air seeped through my clothes and I could feel my lungs ache with the need of something to help warm me.

"Screw you!"

But he wasn't there. My head turned a sharp left and then right. He was gone, had he always been there?

Hunter rushed me abruptly, one hand covering my mouth in a tight grip. The other arm grabbing me at the waist to pull me off my feet and drag me back.

I tried to scream out. I kicked, flailing my arms wildly while trying to elbow him. He pinched my face so tightly as his dirty, sweaty hands that smelled of something foul made the vodka turn in my stomach to reappear.

The air escaped my chest and lungs as he slammed my upper body into a wall. I felt the cold and hard stone. Disoriented, I ached with an intense amount of pressure and pain. My senses were weakened as the contents in my stomach sloshed around and my nerves quivering in my body at my predicament.

Hunter, easily over powered me. He pressed against my body, forcing me up against the wall and a knee parted my legs. This quick maneuver convincing me this was not his first time. This was a planned strategy.

"No!"

I continued to scream over and over. It was muffles cries as his dirty palm covered my mouth.

I tried to elbow and push off the wall, but I couldn't match his strength. All it made him do was chuckle and apply more pressure squeezing my lower jaw. I felt my vocal cords struggle for air.

I could feel the rough edges of the stone cutting into my forehead. I felt him press himself against me. The bile from the vodka sat in my throat. I wanted to throw it up, it would make him back off. My throat burned by the pressure of his hand on my face and I thought at some point I was going to hear a snap of my bones.

His hot breath rested on my neck and traveled up my ear. He was twisted being turned on by this.

"Just remember, I could have you like this. You could scream and no one would come to help. No one would do a thing."

He kissed the back of my neck. With all my strength, I pushed myself off the wall. His strong hand squeezed my cheeks together and pulled my head back. The pain was so intense I thought he was going to squeeze some teeth out. *Headbutt him!* Hunter spun me around and shoved me against the wall hard enough to knock the wind out of me.

My torso and legs weakened. It was his strength holding me up and in place. My lungs fought to catch my breath. The dark stare from his eyes terrified me. He flattened my back against the wall, again, parting my legs with his knees.

"In time, you'll beg me to take you like this," he muttered.

One hand ruffled my skirts to travel up and in between my legs. His fingers stopped as tears ran from my cheeks and onto his hand. This act somehow made him upset. He pushed my right cheek into the wall. I thought with his strong force my neck might snap. I was in too much pain to cry for help. Though, I felt a small part of me welcome death if he was to do it.

His lips touched my right ear. "I think you should shower first. Don't need no dirty wench in my bed."

He pushed off me. I slide down the wall and crashed on my knees. He laughed as he walked away. He casually made his way toward the open exit onto the grounds, and left me alone to pick myself up and trust he wouldn't return to force himself upon me.

Stunned, embarrassed and pissed at my situation. I wrapped my arms around my body and rocked back and forth as I was alone and afraid. The anger and hatred for this place was breaking me.

My voice croaked. "Help." Nothing came out but a sad whisper.

The sound of shuffling of feet, or rustling leaves? My ears perked up and the terror that shook me to my core didn't want me to stick around and wait. My legs wobbled as I struggled. My back smacking against the wall, I slid, disappearing in the darkness of the hallway.

I needed a place to hide, because if I screamed, Hunter could come back and silence me in a way that would be unforgivable.

Even as the sore tips of my fingers ached, they glided down the hallway to help me keep balance. My eyes pooled with water. The LED candles were dimmed, forcing my eyes to adjust to the darkness in the long hall.

My mind raced back to the images of Hunter. How he

laughed at me, grabbed me, smelled me and then kissed the back of my neck. I was wandering around, not knowing where to go.

The smell of lavender was near. My stiff and sore neck glanced up to see a purple stone carved up above. Water puddled inside the room. I knew where I was, the shower stalls on the women's side.

My tired and sore feet ached with each step. The second they touched the heated floor, the spread of the heat was slowly defrosting my feet. The sharp feeling of pin needles from the bottom of my feet seemed angry with the sudden change in temperature made each step challenging.

The adrenaline was wearing off. My body ached and twitched from the pain. The bruises on my arms, stomach and back pulsed as blood rushed to repair the damage that was inflicted upon me.

There wasn't much candle light in the shower stalls. Anyone could have been around. Then again, no one was around. I heard the drip of water echo in the room and the shuffling of my feet as I stepped into the puddles that didn't reach the drain in the middle of the floor.

The water nurtured my feet with moisture. My hands were dirtied, bloody and my apron was torn, dirty which then made me think the rest of my body was. Knowing Hunter's hand reached under my skirts, then thinking about how he squeezed my face. All I could think about was how to make myself clean, rub his touch off my body.

Reaching out and turning the shower stall, arching my neck back, I heard the bones of my neck grind. My face felt sore and squished as my jaw hurt to open.

The warm water didn't make me feel clean enough, I turned up the heat. I grabbed the bar of soap and scrubbed my face. I continuously rubbed and scratched thinking of his dirty hands. The sting reminded me of every second his hands groped my body.

I scrubbed until the lemon and lavender overpowered my senses, and I couldn't smell him any longer. The water temperature was rising, steam surrounded me, I finally was able to fall to my knees and throw up. I lifted my skirts to clean and rub off the areas where I felt his fingers on my thighs. Knowing I felt his arousal tonight made the contents in my stomach finally make their appearance.

My legs buckled, I fell to my knees and threw up the vodka. The hot water poured over my head, my clothes, and with the soap, I scrubbed his disgusting sour scent off me.

My skin tightened as the soap dried out my skin. The few scrapes and cuts I endured from the stone as he pressed my face into the wall, reminded me he touched me. As the water heated and poured out from the shower head. The added weight of my skirts weighed held me down.

The sour smell of vodka burned in my nostrils and was a reminder of the fool I was. The contents were being washed down the drain, but no amount of water could wash away the filth of Hunter's hands.

The water from the shower head turned off. I was over heated and exhausted. My eyes couldn't stay awake, I collapsed on the floor. Then I heard a woman in the faint distance shout for help.

THE NEXT MORNING

I woke up in my bed with a fresh new nightgown and Amara at my bedside checking my pulse. My tired and sore eyes barely open, she sensed I was awake and gave me a faint smile.

"How are you?"

Her voice was gentle and caring. It was in her eyes, I could see she was worried about me. Besides Zak, she was the next friend I had in this God-Forsaken place. She was a protector and had been since day one, just like Zak.

When my lips went to answer, the tightness in my jaw from Hunter's grip on my face suddenly shot back in my memory. My face felt bruised as my finger-tips softly touched my cheeks. I shook my head.

Her shoulders slumped, she grabbed the bowl of food.

"I think you should try." She suggested. "Doc says you need nutrients."

Every muscle in my body ached. I felt my muscles stretch under my skin like I ran a marathon.

"Water." My hoarse voice cracked.

Quickly, Amara grabbed the wooden cup and handed it to

me. I sipped slowly as she suggested. The room temperature water was refreshing on my tongue and rolled easy down my throat. A headache pulsed in the back of my head, my lacking dehydration reminded me all over again how I ended up like this.

My stomach muscles burned as I sat up. I tried not to react, but that felt out of my control. Amara adjusted herself to give me space and pulled the one chair we had in the room, to sit next to my bed. Her hands on her laps, she was waiting for me to say something.

"Where are the twins?" I asked.

"Dining hall, for breakfast." She answered. Her pleading eyes staring at me. Looking down, then back up at me, her lips parted, she wanted to ask me something, but was careful with her words.

"Do you want to talk about where I found you?"

"What did you tell them about me?" I asked.

"You weren't feeling well and had a slight fever. Mother was able to have them temporarily removed so they wouldn't get sick."

I swung my legs over the bed. I gripped my sheets on either side of me staying silent and contemplating. Amara sat back with her hands resting on her thighs. She watched over and nursed me. I should be a better friend to her. I nodded.

AFTER EXPLAINING my time after we separated from the dining hall, to the empty room with the marble compass floor, where Mother's suggested my corrective surgery, then to Aldrich's windmill trip, I tried hard not to end in tears with Hunter's attack. She new everything at this point. I wasn't holding back and relief lifted from my shoulders when I shared with someone about my dilemma.

"That's why you found me in the shower." I finished.

Stunned, she sat and listened to me, holding her hands to her lips at times in shock and the tears pooled in her eyes.

"This needs to stay between me and you." I asked. "My fear involving others would cause more harm than good."

Amara reached over and took my hands in hers.

"I am so sorry you have carried this burden," Amara squeezed gently. "I am your friend, you can count on me. No one else knows you are here."

"How is that possible? You couldn't have carried me up those stairs."

The image of her tiny frame being a She-Hulk was a touch humorous to my imagination, but my muscles tightened in pain at the thought of laughter.

"I didn't. I was looking for you, it was getting dark and I didn't want to worry anyone." She released her gentle grip and sat back. "Mother told me earlier that you were at the windmill. She didn't say why, but that you would come out when you were ready."

Amara crossed her arms over her stomach. I could see in her body language she was uncomfortable remembering what happened.

"I stayed close near the herb garden, waiting for you. Then, I got lost at looking at everything, I thought I might have missed you. So I left."

She rubbed the sides of her arms and squeezed. "I thought I heard a scuffle of something down the slope." Her eyes looking down. "I wandered over and Reynard was talking to Hunter. He seemed heated over something, looking disheveled."

If Hunter was by himself, and Reynard found him, then my harassment with him was over when he left me.

"Reynard asked him where you were. He knew Hunter was to escort you back." Amara reached out to take one of my hands. She delicately traced the scratches on my hand, pressing her lips together as she chin quivered.

"Hunter brushed it off, like it wasn't a big deal. I felt a pain inside my chest." She tapped on her left breast. "Something was wrong, I could feel it." Her voice weakened. "I just ran from them and I needed to find you."

My hand squeezed hers in return. I was the one in pain, but she felt mine as I felt hers.

"You did find me." My throat dried, I could barely say above a whisper.

A tear escaped down her cheek and she quickly wiped it away and sniffled.

"Reynard wasn't far behind. When I found you, I promised him I would watch over you and I didn't want anyone involved. I begged him and then he agreed and we snuck you up here as everyone gathered for dinner."

"How long have I had a fever?" I used the air quotes around the word.

"Last night was the incident and it's almost lunch time now."

"I'm surprised Doctor Ferrarius hasn't made you hook me up to an I.V. or Mother isn't hovering around."

My butt was getting numb. I had been off my feet, getting the sleep I needed. I went to stand and my cracked and blistered feet made me wince in pain. I held onto the bed post and gripped the sides of Amara's bed frame that sat above mine.

Amara wanted to come over and help, but I shook my head.

"Let me do this." I pleaded.

Her hands on her hips, she smacked her tongue to the roof of her mouth.

"Stop trying to do everything alone. I'm here for you."

I nodded as my hand reached out to her, she was at my

side, held one side of my waist and assisted me around the room. After about five minutes, I was on my own, but walking sorely around.

Being in the tight quarters, I was feeling suffocated. I needed fresh air.

"Are you sure, what about Hunter?" Amara asked.

My hands gripped the back of the chair to help me stand to my feet.

Stay strong, Liz. What would Shannon do? What would Brant do?

"I won't lie, I'm terrified to see him." I admitted. "But I can't hide, because I need to find a way out of this place. Sooner than what Mother has offered."

That was it. I made up my mind. I wanted to escape as fast as I could and in the meantime, I would play the part.

GREENHOUSE

When the sun radiated its warm rays on my face, I instantly could feel my skin spread with warmth. It was a beautiful day as the blue sky showed smeared clouds. I would always imagine myself when I was younger taking my thumb up to the sky and as I squinted, I acted like my hand or thumb smeared the clouds.

My lungs inhaled the fresh pine. It was my new favorite smell since I have been here. Smelling the scent reminded me of clean and crisp surroundings.

"Liz!"

With Amara by my side helping me keep the heavy door open, we both shielded our foreheads to see off in the distance two bodies jogging in our direction.

"The twins." Amara told me.

When they approached, they carried a pair of what I had seen in the shoe stores, called slippers. But how they were made of leather and tied with leather string and fur from an animal on the inside. Reminded me of what settlers traded for the winter.

"We were all given moccasins after lunch." Yasmin

approached with an eager smile, then it faded the second she got a good look at my face. "What happened?"

Esther stopped and looked in Amara's direction. "You said it was a fever."

"It was." I chimed in. "I had taken a nasty fall last night from not feel well."

The twins looked at one another, then back at me. They handed me the moccasins.

The soft brown leather was smooth and well secured with the bindings. Inside my hand glided down to feel the soft fur.

"What is the fur?" I asked.

I found a small bench near the area to walk over and sit down on. I wanted to slip on the moccasins. My feet needed the comfort.

"Deer I think." Esther followed. "Size eight, right?"

I nodded and smiled she knew that. "How did you know?"

Esther shrugged her shoulders. "Lucky guess."

The bristles must have been cleaned because it was so soft to slip each foot into.

"I will never take shoes for granted, again."

I sighed with the immediate relief in my feet. My hands still sore and cramped from sewing, I pumped my fists out to work as best as I could from my fingers. I tugged at the tops of my new shoes and pulled up so half my calves were covered. The leather string was strong with a touch of citrus scent to it.

"Helps keep them from drying out." Esther pointed out.

I cupped my palms and inhaled at the citrus scent of oranges. The oil from the leather strings refreshed my senses. I inhaled as much as I could.

A big white fluffy cloud drifted by and blocked the sunlight. My eyes adjusted from squinting to see men and women walking around, going about their business or talking amongst themselves.

The women who are already established here, their skirts had a few extra layers. Their dresses had more of a bodice than a wrap around layer like we had. At least we could distinguish from those who have been here to the new comers.

Over in the greenhouse, women carried baskets at their waists with vegetables. Amara came over from what looked to be a heated disagreement between her and Yasmin.

"Why don't we go pick some herbs for those scratches and I can try and make you a heeling ointment." Amara offered.

Smelling nature in its finest atmosphere seemed refreshing. Both of the twins needed to head into a different direction.

"See you at dinner." Yasmin called back.

I was trying not to limp as I walked. My muscles were not as tight as when I woke up. If I applied pressure, I ached, but walking it off so far was the best medicine.

Amara and I entered the greenhouse and the sweet musk and humidity was like stepping into a chilled version of a sauna. My dry skin felt like a desert as it soaked in the moisture.

The smells of fresh mint as we entered the medicinal area was a deep uniqueness I had only ever known at Christmas. In the city, most people went with already lighted artificial Christmas Trees. It was easier to put up, cleanup was minimal, and it was a one time cost. The downside was, there was no smell beside the plastic bristles that were realistic. So, there was the pine sticks we got to stick in our trees to get that woodsy, Christmas smell.

Amara was at the aloe plants and lavender bushes. She examined them, seeing what could she use to be useful.

"This place must be the mecca of all Greenhouses."

My eyes wandered up and around the filtration system,

watering hoses, carefully sectioned temperature controlled areas. The pine trees already established into the ground were secured with nailed posts of locations of where certain herbs were and other plants.

My eyes couldn't help but catch the beautiful red color of the ripest cherry tomatoes I had ever seen. Not far, the cucumbers were fresh and chilled to the touch.

"You are da new ladies, jes?" A loud deep Italian accent male voice came from the opposite side, as he held a basket of carrots and leak."

From the raspberry vines, as he walked through, the tall well rounded man clipped a vine to carefully place in his wicker basket. His kind dark eyes, prominent thick black eyebrows and matching short thin black hair that curled in a wave made me miss a friend back home.

His beautiful olive skin tone, high cheek bones and even under his full lips, a beautiful and carefully kept mustache that spread down on both side of his lips to meet his chin, he was a handsome man that dressed as a professional chef.

"Halo," the man waved at Amara and myself. The heavy round stature of his torso was oddly paired with a narrow waist and thin legs. His accent was thick, but his eyes and smile was friendly enough to not feel any type of threat.

Amara and I waved back to him. He came over to show us the raspberries.

"Look at deez…bellissime Bacchae." He kissed a berry, looking proud. "I sorry. I mean es to say beautiful berries."

"Amara and this is Liz." Amara suggested between the two of us.

"Ah, jes. I'm Maestro Roberto. I have been in charge of cook de food. Only natural."

"Everything has been delicious." I smiled back.

Maestro Roberto kissed the tips of his fingers on his right

hand in the strong Italian gesture he was pleased with my comment.

"Please stop by anytime. I love de help and I love de teachings." He motioned with his hands.

Maestro Roberto reminded me of a friend back home, Anthony Gallo. A guy I knew back in college at UCLA. We studied together and I loved listening to Anthony's Italian accent and even more so, his Italian cooking.

Remembering my memory with Anthony. How he made me laugh, made me feel like I was his only bella donna. During our senior year, Anthony's family needed him back home in Venice and he asked me to go.

I placed a gentle hand to my heart, not really listening to Maestro Roberto talk to Amara, but I somehow convinced them I was paying attention.

Thinking about Anthony, I wanted to tell him yes, but deep down I was scared and had one more year left in college.

"You cult travel abroad." His wide smile and perfect teeth glimmered at me. "Ah, bella per favore vieni con me."

He was always so tender with his touches. When he leaned in to kiss me, I melted. It was so easy for him to drift along in life and bounce from place to place. That wasn't me and I didn't know how to tell him no.

In fact, I never got to. That night he left with another friend to get us dinner. They were only supposed to be gone a half hour. When I heard the sirens zip by twenty minutes later. Two blocks down, a drunk driver never saw Anthony in the cross walk and struck him.

That was the first time I saw a dead body. I ran over to him, already the gut feeling like I knew, he was gone. I was out of my mind as I ran past the police officer and to Anthony's body. His face was a bloody mess and covered that beautiful Italian skin. His eyes were closed and I would never see his beautiful brown eyes anymore.

Choked up at the memory. I excused myself from Amara and Maestro Roberto as they talked about herbs and remedies. They barely paid me any attention as I left to clear my head and more importantly to mourn for a friend I hadn't thought about in a long time.

A FURRY FRIEND

The sunlight was a warm welcome in the afternoon sun. I stepped down the steps and thought I heard a cry of something on the side of the green house. I followed the sound and came to abrupt stop with Angela.

"Oh!" I was startled as we almost smacked bodies both coming around the sharp corner.

"Angela, I'm so sorry."

The normal resting and constant inquisitive expression she carried didn't change.

"What did," her eyes widened, seeing the scrapes and bruises on my face. Her arms folded onto of her large breasts. Her head titled, clearly examining me.

My eyes shifted and I was not in the mood to rehash and discuss last night. I wanted to step sideways, but she was just as quick on her feet, anticipating my move.

"Who?" Angela asked.

"I was clumsy last night—"

"Who, Liz?" She bit down.

The anger brewing in her chest, straight lips and the attitude of low tolerance made me feel like when I told Shannon the first time I got beat up as a young girl.

My sore throat swallowed and I felt my eye twitch as I tried not to make a sound I was in pain. I didn't want anyone else involved, because I didn't know who to trust or what would happen. I didn't want anyone's blood on my hands.

Angela inhaled deeply through her nostrils and stood her ground waiting for an answer.

"Like I said..." I tried to say.

Angela put her clenched fists at her sides. I know I was upsetting her by with holding what happened.

"I came from a mother who was beaten on a nightly basis. She sneezed, she got beat. She burnt the Mac and cheese, she got beat. She brought the wrong beer—"

"I get it." I interrupted. "It's not like that."

"It never is." She fought between pointing at me or clenching her fist she was so angry. "You allow the person that did this to you have all the power by doing and saying, nothing."

"He's a Watchman." My eyes felt heavy and pooled. "I don't know what power he has."

Angela straightened up her demeanor. "Do you need my help?" Her voice remained calm.

We didn't have to say who it was. She knew by our discussion yesterday. I nodded, she gave me a slight nod in return. It felt like we were having a telepathic exchange of some sort in this moment. We understood with just a nod that something needed to be done.

She had been living on these grounds and lived the Faithful way. I was not familiar, but it was clearly not a direction Angela approved.

"Until then. I will have to see my husband, he said to meet him in the greenhouse." Angela informed me.

"Who's your husband?"

"Roberto. Mi Italiano bello." A thick Italian accent easily slid from her lips.

"He's talking herbs with Amara." I pointed toward the front.

"Oh great." Her New York accent came right back. "He'll be there all night." She walked away.

A FRESH BREEZE drifted by and the smell of grass and hay from the farm consumed my nostrils. I saw the linen cabin and thought about heading up to see if there was socks to try and put my feet into with the moccasins.

"Meow…"

I heard the soft cry of a cat nearby. Shading my vision, I carefully scanned the area. I heard the meow again and with my lips, I pursed them to make soft kissing sounds. My eagerness to find this cat was now top priority, because the thought of having a furry friend excited me.

Landing on all fours in front of me was a white and tan calico cat. It jumped from a nearby branch, rubbing its back against the wood of the cabin and meowed for attention in cute small bursts. Seeing the creature brought a smile to my face, I didn't mind the soreness of my cheeks as they stretched. I kneeled, extending my hand out in the hopes it would come up to me.

The tiny pink nose sniffed my fingers and then rubbed my hand along its jaw line up to it's spine. My fingers dug in and scratched the back of its head. The immediate emotion in my heart was the happiest I had been since my arrival. I loved animals and this ball of cuteness was in need of love and pampering.

Something spooked the cat and it ran away in the direction behind the cabin and into the forest. I picked up my skirts, looking around to figure out what could have spooked the creature.

I dusted off my hands from the fur it shedded, already missing my little friend. I pursed my lips again calling for it. My careful steps looking at the tight spaces it could have ran to. In the back of the cabin, I saw a steep incline and nothing but forest in the great beyond.

I pursed my lips a few more times and nothing. Disappointed I already lost sight of my furry friend, I turned to walk back where I heard the cry of a meow again.

As I spun back around. Not only was it a mistake because of my tight skin and sore muscles, but the pain was easily masked seeing my furry friend sprint up the incline slope. The sounds around me drowned out. I was alone and as far as I was concerned, no one saw me go back here.

The cat sat near the bottom of a tree to turn around and meow at me again. The cat rubbed it's back against the bark and waited for me. Or at least when I picked up my skirts and followed the friendly feline, that's the reasoning that made sense in my head.

After a few long strides, my furry friend stood on top of a boulder and meowed. When I got close, it darted deeper into the forest, heading South. I could feel the change in elevation as I leaned back as my feet carried me at a downward slope. It wasn't steep, but when I glanced back, the top of the greenhouse was slightly visible. I felt the twigs under my shoes and the crunching of the weeds and undisturbed dirt.

This cat was leading me somewhere. I could feel it. I was also extremely superstitious and believed in signs. For the most part, I had ignored most of my gut feeling, but this I wouldn't back down from. I was a believer in fate. I always waited for a sign for something. This time, I made myself follow it.

Through thickets of bushes, hurdling over dead trees, my

furry friend would run up about thirty feet in front of me and then turn around to see if I was following.

The loud sound of snapping twigs from my weight, I was getting fatigued on my journey. I deeply regretted now not eating anything. I'm struggling to match the light footing and stealth sprint of my furry friend's all of maybe four pounds. There was another hill from the grade. The trees began to thin and the crisp air in my lungs made me feel light headed.

Once I caught my breath and bent to rest my hands to my knees, when my breathing shallowed, that's when I could slip back into the time I relied on the sounds from my darkness, my ears perked up at the humming sound.

Standing up, down an embankment, was a camouflage chain link fence. My eyes followed up to the West and then back down to the East. The chain link fence stretched as far as I could see. This must be a start of a perimeter.

Strength came back to me, from a place I couldn't fathom. Hope in my heart, my furry friend and I carefully went down the embankment to approach the fence.

The fence was at least forty feet high as I came closer, the dark green chain link radiated heat. In the branches of the trees, barbed wire rolled across the top. Following down the length to the ground, where I was standing, a piece of the fence was lifted like it had been bent. Underneath was a small hole, like an animal digging up as the fresh dirt disturbed the Earth.

Could a bear or wolf have tried to dig here? I took a few steps closer, the humming became louder and my ears heard the ear piercing sound like a dog whistle.

"Meow..."

My furry friend saw my presence and rubbed up against my legs. I bent down to pick it up, but it scurried and ran into the trench.

In this moment, I could have sworn my heart stopped. "No!"

I looked away, pinched my eyes shut. I waited for the sizzle sound of electrocution. After a few seconds, I peered at the area to see my furry friend on the other side of the fence sitting and licking its paw at me.

"No way." I grabbed a stick and tossed it to the fence and nothing happened.

As my feet carried me closer, my hands stretched out and shook as the tips of my fingers made contact and nothing happened.

I exhaled and gripped the fence. Looking around I couldn't tell where the seam was. My eyes glanced down at the trench, then back out to beyond the green forest down the slope as the beautiful mountain ranges stretched beyond my vision.

There were no signs of a city, no smoke from a chimney, no planes in the sky. It was an eerie silence as the forest and sky stretched far and wide. The sun wasn't far from getting ready to set in the West.

On my knees, I felt the softness of the disturbed dirt, it was easily moveable, but I was nowhere near small enough to crawl under like my feline friend.

Looking behind me, I closed my eyes to drown out the humming and listen to nature guide me. There was a breeze, the whistle through the trees and rustle of leaves. There were no voices, no feet stomping through the woods. No one was looking for me, yet.

It's now or never!

The stick I grabbed before was long and thick. My heart pounding against my chest, I didn't know how much time I had, but I wanted to be out there and not trapped in here. I was going to give myself the chance to get out.

I moved and broke up the dirt as much as I could. I

maneuvered the stick to break up the other side as I stuck the stick through the fence. Once enough soft dirt broke up, I put the stick down to scoop the dirt out of the hole and toss it to the side.

I used every ounce of energy in my lungs with grunts and grinding my teeth as it took a great amount of strength. Over and over my hands grabbed the stick as tight as they could to jam into the dirt, press down and loosen the ground. It was getting tougher, or I was running out of fuel.

I jabbed the stick in and felt warm liquid from my hands, I lost my grip and slipped. My hands grabbed a hold of the fence as I almost fell into the small hole. They were cut and I was bleeding. Ignoring my hands, I pushed myself up, adjusted myself to get ready to jab the stick back in, when it hit a rock, I leaned at the same time, the stick broke and I went down into the hole on my face.

Quickly recovering, because I had no idea how much time I had left. Tossing the stick aside, I would grab as much dirt and would stay here however long it took, or hopefully be on the other side by the time they found me.

The cold pebbles and dirt made my hands ice cold. Sharp pain was no match for the adrenaline racing through my body. I didn't care what damage I did to myself, as long as I could dig myself out.

I was seeing some progress and this made me fight harder and faster. I could feel the freedom just beyond the other side. My body able to sit somewhat in the hole to pull under the fence and claw at the dirt to break up.

The sweat dripped down my face. I felt like the energizer bunny at the speed I worked at. Trying to measure my progress, I got out of the shallow hole to visualize myself getting through.

Pressing my hands to my dress skirts to wipe the blood from my hands. I was willing to sacrifice a few layers if I must. Then, behind me, a twig snapped. My body tensed, I froze in place.

"Don't!"

I heard a man's voice behind me. There was a panic in his tone.

"Miss, you'll get electrocuted," he said. "This fence is turned off for repair, but in forty-five seconds, it will turn back on."

The hard goosebumps formed on my body. My ears knew that voice. I would know that voice better than anyone. I only knew that voice as we shared the darkness together.

On my knees, I slowly turned in his direction.

"Zak?" My hoarse voice quivered.

The man stiffened. His thick black eyebrows raised, his prominent chiseled jaw drops open. His eyes soften.

"Liz?"

TO BE CONTINUED in the second book, titled...Forever Deceitful

THE AUTHOR

Danielle Kathleen is no stranger to story telling. Residing in Reno, Nevada, she loves a good series as characters unfold. Her current works have been in young adult fiction, but this tempting psychological thriller wouldn't leave her alone during the pandemic. She wrote it out back in 2020 and then sat on the idea, waiting for it to emerge.

All Authors have characters nag at them until their stories are told. Three years later during a crazy busy winter/summer season, the stars aligned. She wrote it out, within just a few short months.

Don't be shy, and check her out on her social media page. She loves interactions with fans.

ALSO BY DANIELLE KATHLEEN

Summersville Series:

Summersville

A Never Ending Nightmare

Untold Stories

Made in the USA
Monee, IL
19 October 2023

44795045R00133